HAWAIIAN TALES

A COLLECTION OF CLASSIC HAWAIIAN FOLK TALES

Published by Sophene 2019

Hawaiian Tales was first published in 2019 by Sophene Pty Ltd.

These tales wre originally compiled by King Kalakaua and Thos. G. Thrum.

Selection copyright © by Sophene Pty Ltd 2019.

www.sophenebooks.com

ISBN-13: 978-1-925937-14-5

HAWAIIAN TALES

A COLLECTION OF CLASSIC HAWAIIAN FOLK TALES

CONTENTS

EXPLOITS OF MAUI

SNARING THE SUN

Maui was the son of Hina-lau-ae and Hina, and they dwelt at a place called Makalia, above Kahakuloa, on West Maui. Now, his mother Hina made kapas . And as she spread them out to dry, the days were so short that she was put to great trouble and labor in hanging them out and taking them in day after day until they were dry. Maui, seeing this, was filled with pity for her, for the days were so short that, no sooner had she got her kapas all spread out to dry, than the Sun went down, and she had to take them in again. So he determined to make the Sun go slower. He first went to Wailohi, in Hamakua, on East Maui, to observe the motions of the Sun. There he saw that it rose toward Hana. He then went up on Haleakala, and saw that the Sun in its course came directly over that mountain. He then went home again, and after a few days went to a place called Paeloko, at Waihee. There, he cut down all the coconut-trees, and gathered the fibre of the coconut husks in great quantity. This he manufactured into strong cord. One Moemoe, seeing this, said tauntingly to him: "You will never catch the Sun. You are a lazy nobody."

Maui answered: "When I conquer my enemy, and my desire is attained, I will be your death." So he went up Haleakala again, taking his cord with him. And when the Sun arose directly overhead, he prepared a noose of the cord and, casting it, snared one of the Sun's larger beams and broke it off. And thus he snared and broke off, one after another, all the strong rays of the Sun.

Then he shouted triumphantly: "You are my captive, and

now I will kill you for going so swiftly."

And the Sun said: "Let me live, and you shall see me go more slowly hereafter. Behold, have you not broken off all my strong legs, and left me only the weak ones?"

So the agreement was made, and Maui permitted the Sun to pursue its course, and from that time on it went more slowly; and that is the reason why the days are longer at one season of the year than at another. It was this that gave the name to that mountain, which should properly be called Ale-he-ka-la , and not Haleakala.

When Maui returned from this exploit, he went to find Moemoe, who had reviled him. But that individual was not at home. He went on in his pursuit till he came upon him at a place called Kawaiopilopilo, on the shore to the eastward of the black rock called Kekaa, north of Lahaina. Moemoe dodged him up hill and down, until at last Maui, growing wroth, leaped upon and slew the fugitive. And the dead body was transformed into a long rock, which is there to this day, by the side of the road.

THE ORIGIN OF FIRE

Maui and Hina dwelt together, and to them were born four sons, whose names were Maui-mua, Maui-hope, Maui-kiikii, and Maui-o-ka-lana. These four were fishermen. One morning, just as the edge of the Sun lifted itself up, Maui-mua roused his brethren to go fishing. So they launched their canoe from the beach at Kaupo, on the island of Maui, where they were dwelling, and proceeded to the fishing ground. Having arrived there, they were beginning to fish, when Maui-o-ka-lana saw the light of a fire on the shore they had left, and said to his brethren: "Behold, there is a fire burning. Whose can this fire be?"

And they answered: "Whose, indeed? Let us return to the shore, that we may get our food cooked; but first let us get some fish."

So, after they had obtained some fish, they turned toward the shore; and when the canoe touched the beach, Maui-mua leaped ashore and ran toward the spot where the fire had been burning. Now, the curly-tailed alae were the keepers of the fire; and when they saw him coming they scratched the fire out and flew away. Maui-mua was defeated, and returned to the house to his brothers.

Then said they to him: "How about the fire?"

"How, indeed?" he answered. "When I got there, behold, there was no fire; it was out. I supposed some man had the fire, and behold, it was not so; the alae are the proprietors of the fire, and our bananas are all stolen."

When they heard that, they were filled with anger, and decided not to go fishing again, but to wait for the next appearance of the fire. But after many days had passed without their seeing the fire, they went fishing again, and behold, there was the fire! And so they were continually tantalized. Only when they were out fishing would the fire appear, and when they returned they could not find it.

This was the way of it. The curly-tailed alae knew that Maui and Hina had only these four sons, and if any of them stayed on shore to watch the fire while the others were out in the canoe the alae knew it by counting those in the canoe, and would not light the fire. Only when they could count four men in the canoe would they light the fire. So Maui-mua thought it over, and said to his brothers: "Tomorrow morning, you go fishing, and I will stay ashore. But do you take the calabash and dress it in kapa, and put it in my place in the canoe, and then go out to fish."

They did so, and when they went out to fish the next morning, the alae counted and saw four figures in the canoe, and then they lit the fire and put the bananas on to roast. Before they were fully baked one of the alae cried out: "Our dish is cooked! Behold, Hina has a smart son."

And with that, Maui-mua, who had stolen close to them unperceived, leaped forward, seized the curly-tailed alae and exclaimed: "Now I will kill you, you scamp of an alae! Behold, it is you who are keeping the fire from us. I will be the death of you for this."

Then answered the alae: "If you kill me, the secret dies with me, and you won't get the fire." As Maui-mua began to wring its neck, the alae again spoke, and said: "Let me live, and you shall have the fire."

So Maui-mua said: "Tell me, where is the fire?"

The alae replied: "It is in the leaf of the a-pe plant. "

So, by the direction of the alae, Maui-mua began to rub the leaf-stalk of the a-pe plant with a piece of stick, but the fire would not come. Again he asked: "Where is this fire that you are hiding from me?"

The alae answered: "In a green stick."

And he rubbed a green stick, but got no fire. So it went on, until finally the alae told him he would find it in a dry stick; and so, indeed, he did. But Maui-mua, in revenge for the conduct of the alae, after he had got the fire from the dry stick, said: "Now, there is one thing more to try." And he rubbed the top of the alae's head till it was red with blood, and the red spot remains there to this day.

PELE AND KAHAWALI

In the reign of Kealiikukii, an ancient king of Hawaii, Kahawali, chief of Puna, and one of his favorite companions went one day to amuse themselves with the holua, on the sloping side of a hill, which is still called ka holua ana o Kahawali . Vast numbers of the people gathered at the bottom of the hill to witness the game, and a company of musicians and dancers assembled to add to the amusement of the spectators. The performers began their dance, and amid the sound of drums and the songs of the musicians the sledding of Kahawali and his companion commenced. The hilarity of the occasion attracted the attention of Pele, the goddess of the volcano, who came down from Kilauea to witness the sport. Standing on the summit of the hill in the form of a woman, she challenged Kahawali to slide with her. He accepted the offer, and they set off together down the hill. Pele, less acquainted with the art of balancing herself on the narrow sled than her rival, was beaten, and Kahawali was applauded by the spectators as he returned up the side of the hill.

Before starting again, Pele asked him to give her his papa holua , but he, supposing from her appearance that she was no more than a native woman, said: "No! Are you my wife, that you should obtain my sled?" And, as if impatient at being delayed, he adjusted his papa, ran a few yards to take a spring, and then, with this momentum and all his strength he threw himself upon it and shot down the hill.

Pele, incensed at his answer, stamped her foot on the ground and an earthquake followed, which cracked the hill open. She called, and fire and liquid lava arose, and, assuming her supernatural form, with these irresistible ministers of vengeance, she followed down the hill. When Kahawali reached the bottom, he arose, and on looking behind saw Pele, accompanied by thunder and lightning, earthquake, and streams of burning lava, closely pursuing him. He took up his broad spear that he had stuck in the ground at the beginning of the game, and, accompanied by his friend, fled for his life. The musicians, dancers, and crowds of spectators were instantly overwhelmed by the fiery torrent, which, bearing on its foremost wave the enraged goddess, continued to pursue Kahawali and his companion. They ran till they came to an eminence called Puukea. Here Kahawali threw off his cloak of netted ki leaves and proceeded toward his house near the shore. He met his favorite pig and saluted it by touching noses, then ran to the house of his mother, who lived at Kukii, saluted her by touching noses, and said: "Aloha ino oe, eia ihonei paha oe e make ai, ke ai mainei Pele." (Compassion great to you! Close here, perhaps, is your death; Pele comes devouring.) Leaving her, he met his wife, Kanakawahine, and saluted her. The burning torrent approached, and she said: "Stay with me here, and let us die together." He said: "No; I go, I go." He then saluted his two children, Poupoulu and Kaohe, and said, "Ke ue nei au ia olua." (I grieve for you two.) The lava rolled near, and he ran until he reached a deep chasm. He laid down his spear and walked over on it in safety. His friend called out for his help; he held out his spear over the chasm; his companion took hold of it and he drew him securely over. By this time Pele was coming down the chasm with accelerated motion. He ran till he reached Kula. Here he met his sister, Koai, but had only time to say, "Aloha oe!" (Alas for you!) and then ran onto the shore. His younger brother had just landed from his fishing-canoe, and had hastened to his house to provide for the safety of his family, when Kahawali arrived. He and his friend leaped into the canoe, and with his broad spear paddled out to sea. Pele, perceiving his escape, ran to the shore and hurled after him, with prodigious force, great stones and fragments of rock, which fell thickly around but did not strike his canoe. When he had paddled a short distance from the shore the kumukahi (east wind) sprung up. He fixed his broad spear upright in the canoe, that it might answer the double purpose of mast and sail, and by its aid he soon reached the island of Maui, where they rested one night and then proceeded to Lanai. The next day, they moved on to Molokai, and then to Oahu, the abode of Kolonohailaau, his father, and Kanewahinekeaho, his sister, to whom he related his disastrous perils, and with whom he lived everafter.

HIKU AND KAWELU

Not far from the summit of Hualalai, on the island of Hawaii, in the cave on the southern side of the ridge, lived Hina and her son, the kupua, or demigod, Hiku. All his life, Hiku had lived alone with his mother on this mountain summit, and had never once been permitted to descend to the plains below to see the abodes of men and to learn of their ways. From time to time, his quick ear had caught the sound of the distant hula and the voices of the merrymakers. Often had he wished to see the fair forms of those who danced and sang in those far-off coconut groves. But his mother, more experienced in the ways of the world, had never given her consent. Now, at length, he felt that he was a man, and as the sounds of merry arose on his ears, again he asked his mother to let him go for himself and mingle with the people on the shore. His mother, seeing that his mind was made up to go, reluctantly gave her consent and warned him not to stay too long, but to return in good time. So, taking in his hand his faithful arrow, Pua Ne, which he always carried, he started off.

This arrow was a sort of talisman, possessed of marvellous powers, among which were the ability to answer his call and by its flight to direct his journey.

Thus he descended over the rough clinker lava and through the groves of koa that cover the southwestern flank of the mountain, until, nearing its base, he stood on a distant hill; and consulting his arrow, he shot it far into the air, watching its bird-like flight until it struck on a distant hill above Kailua. To this hill he rapidly directed his steps, and, picking up his arrow in due time, he again shot it into the air. The second flight landed the arrow near the coast of Holualoa, some six or eight miles south of Kailua. It struck on a barren waste of pahoehoe, or lava rock, beside the waterhole of Waikalai, known also as the Wai a Hiku (Water of Hiku), where to this day all the people of that vicinity go to get their water for man and beast.

Here he quenched his thirst, and nearing the village of Holualoa, again shot the arrow, which, instinct with life, entered the courtyard of the alii of Kona, and from among the women who were there singled out the fair princess Kawelu, and landed at her feet. Seeing the noble bearing of Hiku as he approached to claim his arrow, she stealthily hid it and challenged him to find it. Then Hiku called to the arrow, "Pua ne! Pua ne!" and the arrow replied, "Ne!" thus revealing its hiding-place.

This exploit with the arrow and the remarkable grace and personal beauty of the young man quite won the heart of the princess, and she was soon possessed by a strong passion for him, and determined to make him her husband.

With her wily arts she detained him for several days at her home, and when at last he was about to start for the mountain, she shut him up in the house and thus detained him by force. But the words of his mother, warning him not to remain too long, came to his mind, and he determined to break away from his prison. So he climbed up to the roof, and removing a portion of the thatch, made his escape.

When his flight was discovered by Kawelu, the infatuated girl was distracted with grief. Refusing to be comforted, she tasted no food, and ere many days had passed was quite dead. Messengers were despatched who brought back the unhappy Hiku, author of all this sorrow. Bitterly he wept over the corpse of his beloved, but it was now too late; the spirit had departed to the nether world, ruled over by Milu. And now, stung by the reproaches of her kindred and friends for his desertion, and urged on by his real love for the fair one, he resolved to attempt the perilous descent into the nether world and, if possible, to bring her spirit back.

With the assistance of her friends, he collected from the mountain slope a great quantity of the kowali . He also prepared a hollow cocoanut shell, splitting it into two closely fitting parts. Then anointing himself with a mixture of rancid cocoanut and kukui oil, which gave him a very strong corpselike odor, he started with his companions in the well-loaded canoes for a point in the sea where the sky comes down to meet the water.

Arrived at the spot, he directed his comrades to lower him into the abyss called by the Hawaiians the Lua o Milu. Taking with him his cocoanut-shell and seating himself astride of the cross-stick of the swing, or kowali, he was quickly lowered down by the long rope of kowali vines held by his friends in the canoe above.

Soon he entered the great cavern where the shades of the departed were gathered together. As he came among them, their curiosity was aroused to learn who he was. And he heard many remarks, such as "Whew! What an odor this corpse emits!" "He must have been long dead." He had rather overdone the matter of the rancid oil. Even Milu himself, as he sat on the bank watching the crowd, was completely deceived by the stratagem, for otherwise he never would have permitted this bold descent of a living man into his gloomy abode.

The Hawaiian swing, it should be remarked, unlike ours, has but one rope supporting the cross-stick on which the person is seated. Hiku and his swing attracted considerable attention from the lookers-on. One shade in particular watched him most intently; it was his sweetheart, Kawelu. A mutual recognition took place, and with the permission of Milu she darted up to him and swung with him on the kowali. But even she had to avert her face on account of his corpse-like odor. As they were enjoying together this favorite Hawaiian pastime of lele kowali, by a preconcerted signal the friends above were informed of the success of his ruse and were now rapidly drawing them up. At first she was too much absorbed in the sport to notice this. When at length her attention was aroused by seeing the great distance of those beneath her, like a butterfly she was about to flit away, when the crafty Hiku, who was ever on the alert, clapped the cocoanut-shells together, imprisoning her within them, and was then quickly drawn up to the canoes above.

With their precious burden, they returned to the shores of Holualoa, where Hiku landed and at once repaired to the house where still lay the body of his beloved. Kneeling by its side, he made a hole in the great toe of the left foot, into which with great difficulty he forced the reluctant spirit, and in spite of its desperate struggles he tied up the wound so that it could not escape from the cold, clammy flesh in which it was now imprisoned. Then he began to lomilomi, or rub and chafe the foot, working the spirit further and further up the limb.

Gradually, as the heart was reached, the blood began once more to flow through the body, the chest began gently to heave with the breath of life, and soon the spirit gazed out through the eyes. Kawelu was now restored to consciousness, and seeing her beloved Hiku bending tenderly over her, she opened her lips and said: "How could you be so cruel as to leave me?"

All remembrance of the Lua o Milu and of her meeting him there had disappeared, and she took up the thread of consciousness just where she had left it a few days before at death. Great joy filled the hearts of the people of Holualoa as they welcomed back to their midst the fair Kawelu and the hero, Hiku, from whom she was no more to be separated.

THE TOMB OF PUUPEHE:
A LEGEND OF LANAI

One of the interesting localities of tradition, famed in Hawaiian song and story of ancient days, is situate at the southwestern point of the island of Lanai, and known as the Kupapau o Puupehe, or Tomb of Puupehe. At the point indicated, on the leeward coast of the island, may be seen a huge block of red lava about eighty feet high and some sixty feet in diameter, standing out in the sea, and detached from the mainland some fifty fathoms, around which centres the following legend.

Observed from the overhanging bluff that overlooks Puupehe, upon the summit of this block or elevated islet, would be noticed a small inclosure formed by a low stone wall. This is said to be the last resting-place of a Hawaiian girl whose body was buried there by her lover Makakehau, a warrior of Lanai.

Puu Pehe was the daughter of Uaua, a petty chief, one of the dependents of the king of Maui, and she was won by young Makakehau as the joint prize of love and war. These two are described in the Kanikau, or Lamentation, of Puu Pehe, as mutually captive, the one to the other. The maiden was a sweet flower of Hawaiian beauty. Her glossy brown, spotless body "shone like the clear sun rising out of Haleakala." Her flowing, curly hair, bound by a wreath of lehua blossoms, streamed forth as she ran "like the surf crests scudding before the wind." And the starry eyes of the beautiful daughter of Uaua blinded the young warrior, so that he was called Makakehau, or Misty Eyes.

The Hawaiian brave feared that the comeliness of his dear captive would cause her to be coveted by the chiefs of the land. His soul yearned to keep her all to himself. He said: "Let us go to the clear waters of Kalulu. There we will fish together for the kala and the aku, and there I will spear the turtle. I will hide you, my beloved, forever in the cave of Malauea. Or, we will dwell together in the great ravine of Palawai, where we will eat the young of the uwau bird, and we will bake them in ki leaf with the sweet pala fern root. The ohelo berries of the mountains will refresh my love. We will drink of the cool waters of Maunalei. I will thatch a hut in the thicket of Kaohai for our resting-place, and we shall love on till the stars die.

The meles tell of their love in the Pulou ravine, where they caught the bright iiwi birds, and the scarlet apapani. Ah, what sweet joys in the banana groves of Waiakeakua, where the lovers saw naught so beautiful as themselves! But the "misty eyes" were soon to be made dim by weeping, and dimmer, till the drowning brine should close them forevermore.

Makakehau left his love one day in the cave of Malauea while he went to the mountain spring to fill the water-gourds with sweet water. This cavern yawns at the base of the over-hanging bluff that overtops the rock of Puu Pehe. The sea surges far within, but there is an inner space which the expert swimmer can reach, and where Puupehe had often rested and baked the honu'ea or sea turtle, for her absent lover.

This was the season for the *kona*, the terrific storm that comes up from the equator and hurls the ocean in increased volume upon the southern shores of the Hawaiian Islands. Makakehau beheld from the rock springs of Pulou the van-guard of a great kona—scuds of rain and thick mist, rushing with a howling wind, across the valley of Palawai. He knew the storm would fill the cave with the sea and kill his love. He flung aside his calabashes of water and ran down the steep, then across the great valley and beyond its rim he rushed, through the bufferings of the storm, with an agonized heart, down the hill slope to the shore.

The sea was up indeed. The yeasty foam of mad surging waves whitened the shore. The thundering buffet of the charging billows chorused with the howl of the tempest. Ah! where should Misty Eyes find his love in this blinding storm? A rushing mountain of sea filled the mouth of Malauea, and the pent-up air hurled back the invading torrent with bubbling roar, blowing forth great streams of spray. This was a war of matter, a battle of the elements to thrill with pleasure the hearts of strong men. But with one's love in the seething gulf of the whirlpool, what would be to him the sublime cataract? What, to see amid the boiling foam the upturned face, and the dear, tender body of one's own and only poor dear love, all mangled? *You* might agonize on the brink; but Makakehau sprang into the dreadful pool and snatched his murdered bride from the jaws of an ocean grave.

The next day, fishermen heard the lamentation of Makakehau, and the women of the valley came down and wailed over Puupehe. They wrapped her in bright new kapa. They placed upon her garlands of the fragrant na-u (gardenia). They prepared her for burial, and were about to place her in the burial ground of Manele, but Makakehau prayed that he might be left alone one night more with his lost love. And he was left as he desired.

The next day no corpse nor weeping lover were to be found, till after some search Makakehau was seen at work piling up stones on the top of the lone sea tower. The wondering people of Lanai looked on from the neighboring bluff, and some sailed around the base of the columnar rock in their canoes, still wondering, because they could see no way for him to ascend, for every face of the rock is perpendicular or overhanging. The old belief was, that some akua, kanekoa, or keawe-manhili (deities), came at the cry of Makakehau and helped him with the dead girl to the top.

When Makakehau had finished his labors of placing his lost love in her grave and placed the last stone upon it, he stretched out his arms and wailed for Puupehe, thus:

> *"Where are you O Puupehe?*
> *Are you in the cave of Malauea?*
> *Shall I bring you sweet water,*
> *The water of the mountain?*
> *Shall I bring the uwau,*
> *The pala, and the ohelo?*
> *Are you baking the honu*
> *And the red sweet hala?*
> *Shall I pound the kalo of Maui?*
> *Shall we dip in the gourd together?*
> *The bird and the fish are bitter,*
> *And the mountain water is sour.*
> *I shall drink it no more;*
> *I shall drink with Aipuhi,*
> *The great shark of Manele."*

Ceasing his sad wail, Makakehau leaped from the rock into the boiling surge at its base, where his body was crushed in the breakers. The people who beheld the sad scene secured the mangled corpse and buried it with respect in the kupapau of Manele.

AI KANAKA:
A LEGEND OF MOLOKAI

On the leeward side of the island of Molokai, a little to the east of Kaluaaha lies the beautiful valley of Mapulehu, at the mouth of which is located the heiau, or temple, of Iliiliopae, which was erected by direction of Ku-pa, the Moi, to look directly out upon the harbor of Ai-Kanaka, now known as Pukoo. At the time of its construction, centuries ago, Kupa was the Moi, or sovereign, of the district embracing the Ahupuaas, or land divisions, of Mapulehu and Kaluaaha, and he had his residence in this heiau which was built by him and famed as the largest throughout the whole Hawaiian group.

Kupa had a priest named Kamalo, who resided at Kaluaaha. This priest had two boys, embodiments of mischief, who one day while the King was absent on a fishing expedition, took the opportunity to visit his house at the heiau. Finding there the pahu kaeke belonging to the temple, they commenced drumming on it.

Some evil-minded persons heard Kamalo's boys drumming on the Kaeke and immediately went and told Kupa that the priest's children were reviling him in the grossest manner on his own drum. This so enraged the King that he ordered his servants to put them to death. Forthwith they were seized and murdered; whereupon Kamalo, their father, set about to secure revenge on the King.

Taking with him a black pig as a present, he started forth to enlist the sympathy and services of the celebrated seer, or wizard, Lanikaula, living some twelve miles distant at the eastern end of Molokai. On the way thither, at the village of Honouli, Kamalo met a man the lower half of whose body had been bitten off by a shark, and who promised to avenge him provided he would slay some man and bring him the lower half of his body to replace his own. But Kamalo, putting no credence in such an offer, pressed on to the sacred grove of Lanikaula. Upon arrival there Lanikaula listened to his griev- ances but could do nothing for him. He directed him, howev- er, to another prophet, named Kaneakama, at the west end of the island, forty miles distant. Poor Kamalo picked up his pig and travelled back again, past his own home, down the coast to Palaau. Meeting with Kaneakama the prophet direct- ed him to the heiau of Puukahi, at the foot of the *pali*, or prec- ipice, of Kalaupapa, on the windward side of the island, where he would find the priest Kahiwakaapuu, who was a kahu, or steward, of Kauhuhu, the shark god. Once more the poor man shouldered his pig, wended his way up the long ascent of the hills of Kalae to the pali of Kalaupapa, descending which he presented himself before Kahiwakaapuu, and pleaded his cause. He was again directed to go still farther along the wind- ward side of the island till he should come to the Ana puhi (eel's cave), a singular cavern at sea level in the bold cliffs be- tween the valleys of Waikolu and Pelekunu, where Kauhuhu, the shark god, dwelt, and to him he must apply. Upon this away went Kamalo and his pig. Arriving at the cave, he found there Waka and Moo, two kahus of the shark god. "Keep off! Keep off!" they shouted. "This place is kapu. No man can enter here, on penalty of death."

"Death or life," answered he, "it is all the same to me if I can only gain my revenge for my poor boys who have been killed." He then related his story, and his wanderings, adding that he had come to make his appeal to Kauhuhu and cared not for his own life.

"Well," said they to him, "Kauhuhu is away now fishing, but if he finds you here when he returns, our lives as well as yours will pay the forfeit. However, we will see what we can do to help you. We must hide you hereabouts, somewhere, and when he returns trust to circumstances to accomplish your purpose."

But they could find no place to hide him where he would be secure from the search of the god, except the rubbish pile where the offal and scrapings of taro were thrown. They therefore thrust him and his pig into the rubbish heap and covered them over with the taro peelings, enjoining him to keep perfectly still, and watch till he should see eight heavy breakers roll in successively from the sea. He then would know that Kauhuhu was returning from his fishing expedition.

Accordingly, after waiting a while, the eight heavy rollers appeared, breaking successively against the rocks; and sure enough, as the eighth dissolved into foam, the great shark god came ashore. Immediately assuming human form, he began snuffing about the place, and addressing Waka and Moo, his kahus, said to them, "There is a man here." They strenuously denied the charge and protested against the possibility of their allowing such a desecration of the premises. But he was not satisfied. He insisted that there was a man somewhere about, saying, "I smell him, and if I find him you are dead men; if not, you escape." He examined the premises over and over again, never suspecting the rubbish heap, and was about giving up the search when, unfortunately, Kamalo's pig sent forth a squeal which revealed the poor fellow's hiding-place.

Now came the dread moment. The enraged Kauhuhu seized Kamalo with both hands and, lifting him up with the intention of swallowing him, according to his shark instinct, had already inserted the victim's head and shoulders into his mouth before he could speak.

"O Kauhuhu, before you eat me, hear my petition; then do as you like."

"Well for you that you spoke as you did," answered Kauhuhu, setting him down again on the ground. "Now, what have you to say? Be quick about it."

Kamalo then rehearsed his grievances and his travels in search for revenge, and presented his pig to the god.

Compassion arose in the breast of Kauhuhu, and he said, "Had you come for any other purpose I would have eaten you, but as your cause is a sacred one I espouse it, and will revenge it on Kupa the King. You must, however, do all that I tell you. Return to the heiau of Puukahi, at the foot of the pali, and take the priest Kahiwakaapuu on your back, and carry him up the pali over to the other side of the island, all the way to your home at Kaluaaha. Erect a sacred fence all around your dwelling-place, and surround it with the sacred flags of white kapa. Collect black hogs by the lau (four hundred), red fish by the lau, white fowls by the lau, and bide my coming. Wait and watch till you see a small cloud the size of a man's hand arise, white as snow, over the island of Lanai. That cloud will enlarge as it makes its way across the channel against the wind until it rests on the mountain peaks of Molokai back of Mapulehu Valley. Then a rainbow will span the valley from side to side, whereby you will know that I am there, and that your time of revenge has come. Go now, and remember that you are the only man who ever ventured into the sacred precincts of the great Kauhuhu and returned alive."

Kamalo returned with a joyful heart and performed all that had been commanded him. He built the sacred fence around his dwelling; surrounded the inclosure with sacred flags of white kapa; gathered together black hogs, red fish, and white fowls, each by the lau, as directed, with other articles sacred to the gods, such as cocoanuts and white kapas, and then sat himself down to watch for the promised signs of his revenge. Day after day passed until they multiplied into weeks, and the weeks began to run into months.

Finally, one day, the promised sign appeared. The snow white speck of cloud, no bigger than a man's hand, arose over the mountains of Lanai and made its way across the stormy channel in the face of the opposing gale, increasing as it came, until it settled in a majestic mass on the mountains at the head of Mapulehu Valley. Then appeared a splendid rainbow, proudly overarching the valley, its ends resting on the high lands on either side. The wind began to blow; the rain began to pour, and shortly a furious storm came down the doomed valley, filling its bed from side to side with a mad rushing torrent, which, sweeping everything before it, spread out upon the belt of lowlands at the mouth of the valley, overwhelming Kupa and all his people in one common ruin, and washing them all into the sea, where they were devoured by the sharks. All were destroyed except Kamalo and his family, who were safe within their sacred inclosure, which the flood dared not touch, though it spread terror and ruin on every side of them. Wherefore the harbor of Pukoo, where this terrible event occurred, was long known as Ai Kanaka (man eater), and it has passed into a proverb among the inhabitants of that region that "when the rainbow spans Mapulehu Valley, then look out for the Waiakoloa,"a furious storm of rain and wind that sometimes comes suddenly down that valley.

KALIUWAA

SCENE OF THE DEMIGOD KAMAPUAA'S ESCAPE FROM OLOPANA

A few miles east of Laie, on the windward side of the island of Oahu, are situated the valley and falls of Kaliuwaa, noted as one of the most beautiful and romantic spots of the island, and famed in tradition as possessing more than local interest.

The valley runs back some two miles, terminating abruptly at the foot of the precipitous chain of mountains which runs nearly the whole length of the windward side of Oahu, except for a narrow gorge which affords a channel for a fine brook that descends with considerable regularity to a level with the sea. Leaving his horse at the termination of the valley and entering this narrow pass of not over fifty or sixty feet in width, the traveller winds his way along, crossing and recrossing the stream several times, till he seems to be entering into the very mountain. The walls on each side are of solid rock, from two hundred to three hundred, and in some places four hundred feet high, directly overhead, leaving but a narrow strip of sky visible.

Following up the stream for about a quarter of a mile, one's attention is directed by the guide to a curiosity called by the natives a *waa* (canoe). Turning to the right, one follows up a dry channel of what once must have been a considerable stream, to the distance of fifty yards from the present stream. Here one is stopped by a wall of solid rock rising perpendicularly before one to the height of some two hundred feet, and down which the whole stream must have descended in a beautiful fall. This perpendicular wall is worn in by the former action of the water in the shape of a gouge, and in the most perfect manner; and as one looks upon it in all its grandeur, but without the presence of the cause by which it was formed, he can scarcely divest his mind of the impression that he is gazing upon some stupendous work of art.

Returning to the present brook, we again pursued our way toward the fall, but had not advanced far before we arrived at another, on the left hand side of the brook, similar in many respects, but much larger and higher than the one above mentioned. The forming agent cannot be mistaken, when a careful survey is made of either of these stupendous perpendicular troughs. The span is considerably wider at the bottom than at the top, this result being produced by the spreading of the sheet of water as it was precipitated from the dizzy height above. The breadth of this one is about twenty feet at the bottom, and its depth about fourteen feet. But its depth and span gradually diminish from the bottom to the top, and the rock is worn as smooth as if chiselled by the hand of an artist. Moss and small plants have sprung out from the little soil that has accumulated in the crevices, but not enough to conceal the rock from observation. It would be an object worth the toil to discover what has turned the stream from its original channel.

Leaving this singular curiosity, we pursued our way a few yards farther, when we arrived at the fall. This is from eighty to one hundred feet high, and the water is compressed into a very narrow space just where it breaks forth from the rock above. It is quite a pretty sheet of water when the stream is high. We learned from the natives that there are two falls above this, both of which are shut out from the view from below, by a sudden turn in the course of the stream. The perpendicular height of each is said to be much greater than of the one we saw. The upper one is visible from the road on the seashore, which is more than two miles distant, and, judging from information obtained, must be between two and three hundred feet high. The impossibility of climbing the perpendicular banks from below deprived us of the pleasure of farther ascending the stream toward its source. This can be done only by commencing at the plain and following up one of the lateral ridges. This would itself be a laborious and fatiguing task, as the way would be obstructed by a thick growth of trees and tangled underbrush.

The path leading to this fall is full of interest to any one who loves to study nature. From where we leave our horses at the head of the valley and commence entering the mountain, every step presents new and peculiar beauties. The most luxuriant verdure clothes the ground, and in some places the beautifully burnished leaves of the ohia, or native apple-tree, almost exclude the few rays of light that find their way down into this secluded nook. A little farther on, and the graceful bamboo sends up its slender stalk to a great height, mingling its dark, glossy foliage with the silvery leaves of the kukui, or candle-nut; these together form a striking contrast to the black walls which rise in such sullen grandeur on each side.

Nor is the beauty of the spot confined to the luxuriant verdure, or the stupendous walls and beetling crags. The stream itself is beautiful. From the basin at the falls to the lowest point at which we observed it, every succeeding step presents a delightful change. Here, its partially confined waters burst forth with considerable force, and struggle on among the opposing rocks for some distance; there, collected in a little basin, its limpid waves, pure as the drops of dew from the womb of the morning, circle round in ceaseless eddies, until they get within the influence of the downward current, when away they whirl, with a gurgling, happy sound, as if joyous at being released from their temporary confinement. Again, an aged kukui, whose trunk is white with the moss of accumulated years, throws his broad boughs far over the stream that nourishes his vigorous roots, casting a meridian shadow upon the surface of the water, which is reflected back with singular distinctness from its mirrored bosom.

To every other gratification must be added the incomparable fragrance of the fresh wood, in perpetual life and vigor, which presents a freshness truly grateful to the senses. But it is in vain to think of conveying an adequate idea of a scene where the sublime is mingled with the beautiful, and the bold and striking with the delicate and sensitive; where every sense is gratified, the mind calmed, and the whole soul delighted.

Famed as this spot is for its natural scenic attractions, intimated in the foregoing description, its claim of distinction with Hawaiians is indelibly fixed by the traditions of ancient times, the narration of which, at this point, will assist the reader to understand the character of the native mind and throw some light also on the history of the Hawaiians.

Tradition in this locality deals largely with Kamapua'a, the famous demigod whose exploits figure prominently in the legends of the entire group. Summarized, the story is about as follows:

Kamapuaa, the fabulous being referred to, seems, according to the tradition, to have possessed the power of transforming himself into a hog, in which capacity he committed all manner of depredations upon the possessions of his neighbors. He having stolen some fowls belonging to Olopana, who was the King of Oahu, the latter, who was then living at Kaneo-he, sent some of his men to secure the thief. They succeeded in capturing him, and having tied him fast with cords, were bearing him in triumph to the King, when, thinking they had carried the joke far enough, he burst the bands with which he was bound, and killed all the men except one, whom he permitted to convey the tidings to the King. This defeat so enraged the monarch that he determined to go in person with all his force, and either destroy his enemy, or drive him from his dominions. He accordingly, despising ease inglorious,

> Waked up, with sound of conch and trumpet shell,
> The well-tried warriors of his native dell,

at whose head he sought his waiting enemy. Success attending the King's attack, his foe was driven from the field with great loss, and betook himself to the gorge of Kaliuwa'a, which leads to the falls. Here the King thought he had him safe; and one would think so too, to look at the immense precipices that rise on each side, and the falls in front. But the sequel will show that he had a slippery fellow to deal with, at least when he chose to assume the character of a swine; for, being pushed to the upper end of the gorge near the falls, and seeing no other way of escape, he suddenly transformed himself into a hog, and, rearing upon his hind legs and leaning his back against the perpendicular precipice, thus afforded a very comfortable ladder upon which the remnant of the army ascended and made their escape from the vengeance of the King. Possessing such powers, it is easy to see how he could follow the example of his soldiers and make his own escape. The smooth channels before described are said to have been made by him on these occasions; for he was more than once caught in the same predicament. Old natives still believe that they are the prints of his back; and they account for a very natural phenomenon, by bringing to their aid this most natural and foolish superstition.

Many objects in the neighborhood are identified with this remarkable personage, such as a large rock to which he was tied, a wide place in the brook where he used to drink, and a number of trees he is said to have planted. Many other things respecting him are current, but as they do not relate to the matter in hand, it will perhaps suffice to say, in conclusion, that tradition further asserts that Kamapua'a conquered the volcano, when Pele its goddess became his wife, and that they afterward lived together in harmony. That is the reason why there are no more islands formed, or very extensive eruptions in these later days, as boiling lava was the most potent weapon she used in fighting her enemies, throwing out such quantities as greatly to increase the size of the islands, and even to form new ones.

Visitors to the falls, even to this day, meet with evidences of the superstitious awe in which the locality is held by the natives. A party who recently visited the spot state that when they reached the falls they were instructed to make an offering to the presiding goddess. This was done in true Hawaiian style; they built a tiny pile of stones on one or two large leaves, and so made themselves safe from falling stones, which otherwise would assuredly have struck them.

BATTLE OF THE OWLS

The following is a fair specimen of the animal myths current in ancient Hawaii, and illustrates the place held by the owl in Hawaiian mythology.

There lived a man named Kapoi, at Kahehuna, in Honolulu, who went one day to Kewalo to get some thatching for his house. On his way back he found some owl's eggs, which he gathered together and brought home with him. In the evening he wrapped them in ti leaves and was about to roast them in hot ashes, when an owl perched on the fence which surrounded his house and called out to him, "O Kapoi, give me my eggs!"

Kapoi asked the owl, "How many eggs had you?"

"Seven eggs," replied the owl.

Kapoi then said, "Well, I wish to roast these eggs for my supper."

The owl asked the second time for its eggs, and was answered by Kapoi in the same manner. Then said the owl, "O heartless Kapoi! why don't you take pity on me? Give me my eggs."

Kapoi then told the owl to come and take them.

The owl, having got the eggs, told Kapoi to build up a *heiau*, or temple, and instructed him to make an altar and call the temple by the name of Manua. Kapoi built the temple as directed; set kapu days for its dedication, and placed the customary sacrifice on the altar.

News spread to the hearing of Kakuihewa, who was then King of Oahu, living at the time at Waikiki, that a certain man had kapued certain days for his heiau, and had already dedicated it. This King had made a law that whoever among his people should erect a heiau and kapu the same before the King had his temple kapued, that man should pay the penalty of death. Kapoi was thereupon seized, by the King's orders, and led to the heiau of Kupalaha, at Waikiki.

That same day, the owl that had told Kapoi to erect a temple gathered all the owls from Lanai, Maui, Molokai, and Hawaii to one place at Kalapueo. All those from the Koolau districts were assembled at Kanoniakapueo, and those from Kauai and Niihau at Pueohulunui, near Moanalua.

It was decided by the King that Kapoi should be put to death on the day of Kane. When that day came, at daybreak the owls left their places of rendezvous and covered the whole sky over Honolulu; and as the King's servants seized Kapoi to put him to death, the owls flew at them, pecking them with their beaks and scratching them with their claws. Then and there was fought the battle between Kakuihewa's people and the owls. At last the owls conquered, and Kapoi was released, the King acknowledging that his Akua (god) was a powerful one. From that time the owl has been recognized as one of the many deities venerated by the Hawaiian people.

KANEAUKAI:
A LEGEND OF WAIALUA

Long ago, when the Hawaiians were in the darkness of super-stition and kahunaism, with their gods and lords many, there lived at Mokuleia, Waialua, two old men whose business it was to pray to Kaneaukai for a plentiful supply of fish. These men were quite poor in worldly possessions, but given to the habit of drinking a potion of awa after their evening meal of poi and fish.

The fish that frequented the waters of Mokuleia were the aweoweo, kala, manini, and many other varieties that find their habitat inside the coral reefs. Crabs of the white variety burrowed in the sand near the seashore and were dug out by the people, young and old. The squid also were speared by the skilful fishermen, and were eaten stewed, or salted and sun-dried and roasted on the coals. The salt likely came from Kaena Point, from salt-water evaporation in the holes of rocks so plentiful on that stormy cape. Or it may have been made on the salt pans of Paukauwila, near the stream of that name, where a few years ago this industry existed on a small scale.

But to return to our worshippers of Kaneaukai. One morning on going out upon the seashore they found a log of wood, somewhat resembling the human form, which they took home and set in a corner of their lowly hut, and contin-ued their habit of praying to Kaneaukai. One evening, after having prepared a scanty supper of poi and salt, with perhaps a few roasted kukui-nuts, as a relish, and a couple of cocoanut cups of awa as their usual drink, they saw a handsome young man approaching, who entered their hut and saluted them. He introduced himself by saying, "I am Kaneaukai to whom you have been praying, and that which you have set up is my image; you have done well in caring for it."

He sat down, after the Hawaiian custom, as if to share their evening meal, which the two old men invited him to partake of with them, but regretted the scanty supply of awa. He said: "Pour the awa back into the bowl and divide into three." This they did and at once shared their meal with their guest.

After supper Kaneaukai said to the two old men, "Go to Keawanui and you will get fish enough for the present." He then disappeared, and the fishermen went as instructed and obtained three fishes; one they gave to an old sorceress who lived near by, and the other two they kept for themselves.

Soon after this there was a large school of fish secured by the fishermen of Mokuleia. So abundant were the fish that after salting all they could, there was enough to give away to the neighbors; and even the dogs had more than they desired.

Leaving the Mokuleia people to the enjoyment of their unusual supply of fish, we will turn to the abode of two kahunas, who were also fishermen, living on the south side of Waimea Valley, Oahu. One morning, being out of fish, they went out into the harbor to try their luck, and casting their net they caught up a calcareous stone about as large as a man's head, and a pilot fish. They let the pilot fish go, and threw the stone back into the sea. Again they cast their net and again they caught the stone and the pilot fish; and so again at the third haul. At this they concluded that the stone was a representative of some god. The elder of the two said: "Let us take this stone ashore and set it up as an idol, but the pilot fish we will let go." So they did, setting it up on the turn of the bluff on the south side of the harbor of Waimea. They built an inclosure about it and smoothed off the rocky bluff by putting flat stones from the immediate neighborhood about the stone idol thus strangely found.

About ten days after the finding of the stone idol the two old kahunas were sitting by their grass hut in the dusk of the evening, bewailing the scarcity of fish, when Kaneaukai himself appeared before them in the guise of a young man. He told them that they had done well in setting up his stone image, and if they would follow his directions they would have a plentiful supply of fish. Said he, "Go to Mokuleia, and you will find my wooden idol; bring it here and set it up alongside of my stone idol." But they demurred, as it was a dark night and there were usually quicksands after a freshet in the Kamananui River. His answer was, "Send your grandsons." And so the two young men were sent to get the wooden idol and were told where they could find it.

The young men started for Mokuleia by way of Kaika, near the place where salt was made a few years ago. Being strangers, they were in doubt about the true way, when a meteor (hoku kaolele) appeared and went before them, showing them how to escape the quicksands. After crossing the river they went on to Mokuleia as directed by Kaneaukai, and found the wooden idol in the hut of the two old men. They shouldered it, and taking as much dried fish as they could carry, returned by the same way that they had come, arriving at home about midnight.

The next day the two old kahunas set up the wooden idol in the same inclosure with the stone representative of Kaneaukai. The wooden image has long since disappeared, having been destroyed, probably, at the time Kaahumanu made a tour of Oahu after her conversion to Christianity, when she issued her edict to burn all the idols. But the stone idol was not destroyed. Even during the past sixty years offerings of roast pigs are known to have been placed before it. This was done secretly for fear of the chiefs, who had published laws against idolatry.

Accounts differ, various narrators giving the story some embellishments of their own. So good a man as a deacon of Waialua in telling the above seemed to believe that, instead of being a legend it was true; for an old man, to whom he referred as authority, said that one of the young men who went to Mokuleia and brought the wooden idol to Waimea was his own grandfather.

An aged resident of the locality gives this version: Following the placement of their strangely found stone these two men dreamed of Kaneaukai as a god in some far-distant land, to whom they petitioned that he would crown their labors with success by granting them a plentiful supply of fish. Dreaming thus, Kaneaukai revealed himself to them as being already at their shore; that the stone which they had been permitted to find and had honored by setting up at Kehauapuu, was himself, in response to their petitions; and since they had been faithful so far, upon continuance of the same, and offerings thereto, they should ever after be successful in their fishing. As if in confirmation of this covenant, this locality has ever since been noted for the periodical visits of schools of the anae-holo and kala, which are prevalent from April to July, coming, it is said, from Ohea, Honuaula, Maui, by way of Kahuku, and returning the same way.

So strong was the superstitious belief of the people in this deified stone that when, some twenty years ago, the road supervisor of the district threw it over and broke off a portion, it was prophesied that Kaneaukai would be avenged for the insult. And when shortly afterward the supervisor lost his position and removed from the district, returning not to the day of his death; and since several of his relatives have met untimely ends, not a few felt it was the recompense of his sacrilegious act.

FISH STORIES AND SUPERSTITIONS

The following narration of the different fishes here is told and largely believed in by native fishermen. All may not agree as to particulars in this version, but the main features are well known and vary but little. Some of these stories are termed mythical, in others the truth is never questioned, and together they have a deep hold on the Hawaiian mind. Further and confirmatory information may be obtained from fishermen and others, and by visiting the market the varieties here mentioned may be seen almost daily.

In the olden time certain varieties of fish were tabooed and could not be caught at all times, being subject to the kapu of Ku-ula, the fish god, who propagated the finny tribes of Hawaiian waters. While deep sea fishing was more general, fishing in the shallow sea, or along shore, was subject to the restrictions of the konohiki of the land, and aliis , both as to certain kinds and periods. The sign of the shallow sea kapu was the placing of branches of the hau tree all along the shore. The people seeing this token of the kapu respected it, and any violation thereof in ancient times was said to be punishable by death. While this kapu prevailed the people resorted to the deep sea stations for their food supply. With the removal of the hau branches, indicating that the kapu was lifted, the people fished as they desired, subject only to the makahiki taboo days of the priest or alii, when no canoes were allowed to go out upon the water.

The first fish caught by a fisherman, or any one else, was marked and dedicated to Ku-ula. After this offering was made, Ku-ula's right therein being thus recognized, they were free from further oblations so far as that particular variety of fish was concerned. All fishermen, from Hawaii to Niihau, observed this custom religiously. When the fishermen caught a large supply, whether by the net, hook, or shell, but one of a kind, as just stated, was reserved as an offering to Ku-ula; the remainder was then free to the people.

DEIFIED FISH SUPERSTITION

Some of the varieties of fish we now eat were deified and prayed to by the people of the olden time, and even some Hawaiians of to-day labor under like superstition with regard to sharks, eel, o'opus , and some others. They are afraid to eat or touch these lest they suffer in consequence; and this belief has been perpetuated, handed down from parents to children, even to the present day. The writer was one of those brought up to this belief, and only lately has eaten the kapu fish of his ancestors without fearing a penalty therefor.

STORY OF THE ANAE-HOLO

The anae-holo is a species of mullet unlike the shallow water, or pond, variety; and the following story of its habit is well known to any kupa (native) of Oahu.

The home of the anae-holo is at Honouliuli, Pearl Harbor, at a place called Ihuopalaai. They make periodical journeys around to the opposite side of the island, starting from Puuloa and going to windward, passing successively Kumumanu, Kalihi, Kou, Kalia, Waikiki, Kaalawai and so on, around to the Koolau side, ending at Laie, and then returning by the same course to their starting-point. This fish is not caught at Waianae, Kaena, Waialua, Waimea, or Kahuku because it does not run that way, though these places are well supplied with other kinds. The reason given for this is as follows:

Ihuopalaai had a Ku-ula, and this fish god supplied anaes. Ihuopalaai's sister took a husband and went and lived with him at Laie, Koolauloa. In course of time a day came when there was no fish to be had. In her distress and desire for some she bethought herself of her brother, so she sent her husband to Honouliuli to ask Ihuopalaai for a supply, saying: "Go to Ihuopalaai, my brother, and ask him for fish. If he offers you dried fish, refuse it by all means; do not take it, because the distance is so long that you would not be able to carry enough to last us for any length of time."

When her husband arrived at Honouliuli he went to Ihuopalaai and asked him for fish. His brother-in-law gave him several large bundles of dried fish, one of which he could not very well lift, let alone carry a distance. This offer was refused and reply given according to instruction. Ihuopalaai sat thinking for some time and then told him to return home, saying: "You take the road on the Kona side of the island; do not sit, stay, nor sleep on the way till you reach your own house."

The man started as directed, and Ihuopalaai asked Ku-ula to send fish for his sister, and while the man was journeying homeward as directed a school of fish was following in the sea, within the breakers. He did not obey fully the words of Ihuopalaai, for he became so tired that he sat down on the way; but he noticed that whenever he did so the fish rested too. The people seeing the school of fish went and caught some of them. Of course, not knowing that this was his supply, he did not realize that the people were taking his fish. Reaching home, he met his wife and told her he had brought no fish, but had seen many all the way, and pointed out to her the school of anae-holo which was then resting abreast of their house. She told him it was their supply, sent by Ihuopalaai, his brother-in-law. They fished, and got all they desired, whereupon the remainder returned by the same way till they reached Honouliuli where Ihuopalaai was living. Ever afterward this variety of fish has come and gone the same way every year to this day, commencing some time in October and ending in March or April.

Expectant mothers are not allowed to eat of the anae-holo, nor the aholehole, fearing dire consequences to the child, hence they never touch them till after the eventful day. Nor are these fish ever given to children till they are able to pick and eat them of their own accord.

MYTH OF THE HILU

The hilu is said to have once possessed a human form, but by some strange event its body was changed to that of a fish. No knowledge of its ancestry or place of origin is given, but the story is as follows:

Hilu-ula and Hilu-uli were born twins, one a male and the other a female. They had human form, but with power to assume that of the fish now known as hilu. The two children grew up together and in due time when Hilu-uli, the sister, was grown up, she left her brother and parents without saying a word and went into the sea, and, assuming her fish form, set out on a journey, eventually reaching Heeia, Koolaupoko. During the time of her journey she increased the numbers of the hilu so that by the time they came close to Heeia there was so large a school that the sea was red with them. When the people of Heeia and Kaneohe saw this, they paddled out in their canoes to discover that it was a fish they had never seen nor heard of before. Returning to the shore for nets, they surrounded the school and drew in so many that they were not able to care for them in their canoes. The fishes multiplied so rapidly that when the first school was surrounded and dragged ashore, another one appeared, and so on, till the people were surfeited. Yet the fish stayed in the locality, circling around. The people ate of them in all styles known to Hawaiians; raw, lawalued, salted, and broiled over a fire of coals.

While the Koolau people were thus fishing and feasting, Hilu-ula, the brother, arrived among them in his human form; and when he saw the hilu-uli broiling over the coal fire he recognized the fish form of his sister. This so angered him that he assumed the form of a whirlwind and entered every house where they had hilu and blew the fish all back into the sea. Since then the hilu-uli has dark scales, and is well known all over the islands.

THE HOU, OR SNORING FISH

The hou lives in shallow water. When fishing with torches on quiet, still nights, if one gets close to where it is sleeping I will be heard to snore as if it were a human being. This is a small beautifully colored fish. Certain sharks also, sleeping in shallow water, can be heard at times indulging in the same habit.

There are many kinds of fish known to these islands, and other stories connected with them, which, if gathered together, would make an interesting collection of yarns as "fishy" as any country can produce.

LONO AND KAIKILANI

I.

What a hustling and barbaric little world in themselves were the eight habitable islands of the Hawaiian archipelago before the white man came to rouse the simple but warlike islanders from the dream they had for centuries been living! Up to that time their national life had been a long romance, abundant in strife and deeds of chivalry, and scarcely less bountiful in episodes of love, friendship and self-sacrifice. Situated in mid-ocean, their knowledge of the great world, of which their island dots on the bosom of the Pacific formed but an infinitesimal portion, did not reach beyond a misty Kahiki, from which their fathers came some centuries before, and the bare names of other lands marking the migratory course of their ancestors thither.

The Hawaiians were barbarous, certainly, since they slew their prisoners of war, and to their gods made sacrifice of their enemies; since no tie of consanguinity save that of mother and son was a bar to wedlock; since murder was scarcely a crime, and the will of the alii-nui on every island was the supreme law; since the masses were in physical bondage to their chiefs and in mental slavery to the priesthood. Yet, with all this, they were a brave, hospitable and unselfish people. The kings of the islands of Hawaii, Maui, Oahu and Kauai were in almost continual warfare with each other until brought under one government by Kamehameha I; but the fear of foreign invasion never disturbed them, and the people, who feared their gods, reverenced their rulers and possessed an easy and unfailing means of sustenance and personal comfort, were content with a condition which had been theirs for generations and was hopeless of amelioration; for the high chiefs in authority claimed a lineage distinct from that of the masses, and between them frowned a gulf socially and politically impassable.

The Hawaiians were never cannibals. The most conspicuous of their barbarisms was the sacrifice of human beings to their gods; but did not the temples of early Gaul and Saxon flow with the blood of men? and did not one of the fathers of Israel sharpen his knife to slay the body of his son upon the altar of the God of Abraham? They knew but little of the arts as we know them now, and the useful and precious metals were all unknown to them; yet they made highways over the precipices, reared massive walls of stone around their temples, carried effective weapons into battle, and constructed capacious single and double canoes and barges, which they navigated by the light of the stars. They had no language either of letters or symbolism, but so accurately were their legends preserved and transmitted that the great chiefs were able to trace their ancestry back, generation by generation, to something like a kinship with the children of Jacob, and even beyond in the same manner to Noah, and thence to Adam. What wonder, then, that under their old kings the islands of Hawaii should have been the home of romance, and that the south wind should have sighed in numbers through the caves of Kona?

And now, borne by the soft breath of the tropics, let us be wafted to the island of Hawaii, and backward over a misty bridge of historic meles to the reign of Kealiiokoloa, a son of Umi and grandson of the famed Liloa. It was during his brief reign—extending, perhaps, from 1520 to 1530—that for a second time a white face was seen by the Hawaiians. A Spanish vessel from the Moluccas was driven upon the reefs of Keei, in the district of Kona, and completely destroyed. But two persons were saved from the wreck—the captain and his sister. They were first thought to be gods by the simple islanders; but as their first request was for food, which they ate with avidity, and their next for rest, which seemed to be as necessary to them as to other mortals, they were soon relieved of their celestial attributes and conducted to the king, who received them graciously and took them under his protection. The captain—named by the natives Kukanaloa—wedded a dusky maiden of good family, and the sister became the wife of a chief in whose veins ran royal blood.

On the death of Kealiiokoloa his younger brother, Keawenui, assumed the sceptre in defiance of the right of Kukailani, his nephew and son of the dead king, who was too young to assert his authority. This he was the better enabled to do in consequence of the sudden death of the king, possibly by poison, before his successor had been formally named. Keawenui's usurpation, however, was resisted by the leading chiefs of the island, who refused to recognize his authority and rose in arms against him. But he inherited something of the martial prowess of his father, Umi, and, meeting the revolted chiefs before they had time to properly organize their forces, destroyed them in detail, and thereafter reigned in peace. Nor could it well have been otherwise, for the bones of the rebellious chiefs of Kohala, Hamakua, Hilo, Puna, Kau and Kona were among the trophies of his household, and Kukailani, lacking ambition, was content with the lot of idleness and luxury which the crafty uncle placed at his command.

And thus, while Keawenui continued in the moiship of Hawaii, Kukailani, the rightful ruler, grew to manhood around the court of his uncle. In due time the prince married, and among the children born to him was Kaikilani, the heroine of this little story. At the age of fifteen she was the most lovely of the maidens of Hawaii. Her face was fairer than any other in Hilo, to which place Keawenui had removed his court; and that is saying much, for the king was noted for his gallantries, and the handsomest women in the kingdom were among his retainers. If her complexion was a shade lighter than that of others, it was because of the Castilian blood that had come to her through her grandmother, the sister of Kukanaloa, and brighter eyes than hers never peered through the lattices of the Guadalquivir.

Kaikilani became the wife of the king's eldest son, Kanaloa-kuaana, and, in further atonement of the wrong he had done her father, on his death-bed Keawenui formally conferred upon her the moiship of Hawaii. Among the other sons left by Keawenui at his death was Lono. His full name was Lonoikamakahiki. His mother was Haokalani, in whose veins ran the best blood of Oahu.

Early in life Lono exhibited remarkable intelligence, and as he grew to manhood, after the death of his father, in athletic and warlike exercises and other manly accomplishments he had not a peer in all Hawaii. So greatly was he admired by the people, and so manifestly was he born to rule, that his brother, the husband and adviser of the queen, recommended that he be elevated to the moiship, in equal power and dignity with Kaikilani.

What followed could have occurred only in Hawaii. A day was appointed for a public trial of Lono's abilities before the assembled chiefs of the kingdom. Although but twenty-three years of age, his knowledge of warfare, of government, of the unwritten laws of the island and the prerogatives of the tabu was found to be complete; and Kawaamaukele, the venerable high-priest of Hilo, whose white hairs swept his knees, and who had foretold Lono's future when a boy, bore testimony to his thorough mastery of the legendary annals of the people and his zeal in the worship of the gods.

So much for his mental acquirements. To test his physical accomplishments the chiefs most noted for their skill, strength and endurance were summoned from all parts of the kingdom. It was a tournament in which one man threw down the glove to every chief in Hawaii. The various contests continued for ten consecutive days, in the presence of thousands of people, and between the many trials of strength and skill were interspersed feasting, music and dancing. The scene was brilliant. More than a hundred distinguished chiefs, in yellow mantles and helmets, presented themselves to test the prowess of Lono in exercises in which they individually excelled. But the mighty grandson of Umi vanquished them all. He outran the fleetest, as well on the plain as in bringing a ball of snow from the top of Mauna Kea. On a level he leaped the length of two long war-spears, and in uli-maita, holua and other athletic games he found no rival. In a canoe contest he distanced twelve competitors, and then plunged into the sea with a pahoa in his hand, and slew and brought to the surface the body of a large shark. He caught in his hands twenty spears hurled at him in rapid succession by as many strong arms, and in the moku-moku, or wrestling contests, he broke the limbs of three of his adversaries.

Among the witnesses of these contests was the still young and comely Kaikilani. It is true that she had frequently met the young hero, and regarded him with such favor as she might the brother of her husband; but now, at the end of his victories, he appeared to her almost as a god, with whom it would be an honor to share the sovereignty of the kingdom; and when, amidst the plaudits of thousands, she threw the royal mamo over his shoulders with her own hands, and in doing so kissed his cheek, her husband saw that she loved Lono better than she had ever loved him. "The gods have decreed it," said Kanaloa, in sorrow, but with no feeling of bitterness, "and so shall it be!"

He consulted with the chiefs and high-priest, and at the conclusion of a feast the same evening, given in honor of Lono, he took his brother by the hand and led him to the apartment of the queen. As they entered, Kaikilani rose from a soft couch of kapa, and waited to hear the purpose of their visit; for it was near the middle of the night, and but a single kukui torch was burning in front of the door. The heart of Kanaloa fluttered in his throat, but he finally said, with apparent calmness:

"My good Kaikilani, what I am about to say is in sorrow to myself and in affection for you. Of all the sons of our father, Lono seems most to have the favor of the gods. Is it strange, then, that he should have yours as well? It is therefore deemed best by the gods, the chiefs and myself that you accept Lono as your husband, and share with him henceforth the government of Hawaii. Is it your will that this be done?"

Kaikilani was almost dazed with the abrupt announcement; but she understood its full meaning, and, after gazing for a moment into the face of Lono and reading no objection there, she found the courage to answer:

"Since it is the will of the gods, it is also mine."

"So shall it be made known by the heralds," said Kanaloa, bowing to hide his grief, and leaving Lono and the queen together.

Thus it was that Lono, of whom tradition relates so many romantic stories, became the moi of Hawaii and the husband of the most attractive woman of her time, Queen Kaikilani.

II.

Peace and prosperity followed the elevation of Lono to the throne of Hawaii. His fame as an able and sagacious ruler soon spread to the other islands of the group, and his court as well as his person commanded the highest respect of his subjects. Weary of inaction, and having no desire to embroil the kingdom in a foreign war, he at length concluded to visit some of the neighboring islands with his queen, and particularly Kauai, which he had once seen when a boy.

Leaving the government in charge of his brother Kanaloa, Lono embarked on his journey of pleasure with a number of large double canoes and a brilliant retinue. He took with him pololous, kahilis and other emblems of state, and the hokeo, or large calabash, containing the bones of the six rebellious chiefs slain by his royal father at the beginning of his reign.

The double canoe provided for Kaikilani and her personal attendants was fitted out in a manner becoming the rank of its royal occupant. It was eighty feet in length, and the two together were seven feet in width. Midway between stem and stern a continuous flooring covered both canoes, which was enclosed to a height of six feet, thus providing the queen with a room seven feet broad and twenty feet in length. The apartment was abundantly supplied with cloths and mats of brilliant colors, and the walls were decorated with festoons of shells and leis of flowers and feathers. In front of the entrance stood two kahilis, and behind a kapa screen was a carved image of Ku, surrounded by a number of charms and sacred relics. The canoes were brightly painted in alternate lines of black and yellow, while above their ornamented prows towered the carved and feathered forms of two gigantic birds with human heads. Forty oarsmen comprised the crew, and sails of mats were ready to lift into every favoring breeze.

The double canoe of the king was smaller and less elaborately ornamented; and as it moved out of the harbor of Hilo, bearing the royal ensign and followed by the sumptuous barge of the queen and the humbler crafts of servants and retainers, the shores were lined with people, and hundred in canoes paddled after them to give them their parting alohas beyond the reef. The auguries had not been favorable. So said the high-priest, and so had the people whispered to each other. But, after preparing for the journey, Lono could not be persuaded to relinquish it. It was therefore with misgivings that he was seen to depart; and for many days thereafter sacrifices were offered for him in the temples, and a strict tabu was ordered for a period of three days, during which time no labor was performed and a solemn silence prevailed over all the land embraced in the dread edict. Swine were confined, fires were extinguished, dogs were muzzled, fowls were hidden under calabashes, and the priests alone were seen and heard, and they but sparingly. Such was the strict tabu for the propitiation of the gods in case of emergency or peril, and death was the certain penalty of its violation.

The weather was fair, and the royal party first stopped at Lahaina. It had been Lono's purpose to spend a week or more at the court of Kamalalawalu, but the moi was absent at the time, and the squadron left Maui the next day for Oahu. A fair wind wafted the party through Pailolo channel to the western point of Molokai. The sky was clear, and Lono began to discern the tops of the mountains of eastern Oahu, when one of his nephews threw his spear into and wounded a large shark which for some time had been slowly moving around the bows of the canoe. In an instant the weapon was thrown back with a violence which drove the point through the rim of the boat. Blood tinged the waves, but the shark disappeared.

Before Lono could recover from his astonishment a furious wind rose from the south and west, and the fleet was driven around to the north side of Molokai, and finally succeeded in effecting a landing at Kalaupapa. Two of the canoes were destroyed during the gale, and the thoughtless young chief who cast the spear was washed into the sea and devoured by a school of black sharks before assistance could reach him. Landing with his party, Lono learned from a priest the cause of the disaster that had overtaken him. It was the god Moaalii, who had taken his characteristic form of a shark and was guiding the fleet to Oahu, that had been wounded by Lono's nephew.

The weather continued boisterous for some days, and Lono and his party became the guests of the chiefs of Kalaupapa. It was not a very inviting spot, and to beguile the time Lono and Kaikilani amused themselves with the game of konane, played upon a checkered board and closely resembling the game of draughts. One day, when thus occupied in the shade of a palm near the foot of an abrupt hill, Lono heard a voice above them. He gave but little attention to it until the name of Kaikilani was pronounced. He listened without raising his head, and soon heard the voice repeat:

"Ho, Kaikilani! Your lover, Heakekoa, is waiting for you!"

Lono looked up, but could see no one above them. He

inquired the meaning of such words addressed to the wife of the moi of Hawaii; but the queen, seemingly confused, was either unable or unwilling to offer any explanation. Enraged at what he hastily conceived to be an evidence of her infidelity, Lono seized the konane board and struck her senseless and bleeding to the earth. Without waiting to learn the result of his barbarous blow, Lono strode to the beach, and, ordering his canoe launched, set sail at once for Oahu, without leaving any orders for the remainder of the fleet.

As he shoved from the shore Kaikilani approached, and, holding out her blood-stained hands, pitifully implored him to remain or take her with him; but he waved her back in anger and resolutely put out to sea. She watched the canoe of her impetuous husband until it became a speck in the distance, and then with a despairing moan sank senseless upon the sands.

Kaikilani was tenderly borne to her domicile by her attendants, and for nine days struggled with a fever which threatened her life. During all that time she tasted neither fish nor poi, but in her delirium appealed continually to Lono, declaring that no one had called to her from the cliffs. On the tenth day her mind was clear and she partook of food, and then on her hands and knees a young woman crawled to the side of her kapa-moe, and, having permission to speak, said:

"O queen, I am the innocent cause of your misery, and my heart breaks for you. I am the daughter of the chief Keeokane, and he has sent me to you. Heakekoa loves me, and it was my name, Kaikinane, that he called from the cliffs, and not yours. It is better that confusion should come to me than shame and grief to the queen of Hawaii."

Kaikilani admonished her attendants to remember the

words of the girl, that they might be able, if necessary, to re-peat them to Lono, and then dismissed her with presents and a promise to speak kindly of her to her father, who was greatly annoyed at the distress which the indiscretion of his daughter had brought to their distinguished guest.

As soon as she had sufficiently recovered, Kaikilani, not knowing what had become of her husband, sorrowfully returned to Hawaii in the hope of finding him there and ex-plaining away the cause of his anger. But the news of Lono's assault upon her and his sudden departure from Molokai had preceded her, probably through the return of some of the ca-noes of the fleet, and when she arrived at Kohala she found the kingdom in a state of rebellion.

With the avowed intent of slaying Lono, should he return to Hawaii, Kanaloa had assumed the regency, supported by the principal chiefs of the island, the relatives of the queen, and all the brothers of Lono with the exception of Pupuakea, a stalwart and warlike son of Keawenui by an humble mother unnamed in the royal annals, and who had large possessions in the district of Kau.

But Kaikilani still loved her hot-headed but instinctive-ly generous husband, and refused to give countenance to the revolt raised in her behalf. She therefore hastily left Kohala at night, and, so sailing as to escape the observation of the rebels, suddenly appeared off the coast of Kau and placed her-self in communication with Pupuakea, the only chief of note that still adhered to the fortunes of Lono. He had succeeded in rallying to the support of his cause a very considerable force, but he knew that it would avail him little against the united armies of the opposition, and after a full consideration of the situation it was decided that Pupuakea should remain on the defensive until the return of Lono, of whom Kaikilani resolved to go at once in search.

With this understanding Kaikilani, inspired by the hope of winning back her husband's love, after a few preparations started on her errand; but not before she had made sacrifices to the gods and implored their assistance, and Pupuakea brought word to her from the temple that the auguries of her journey showed a line of dark clouds ending in sunshine. But what cared she for clouds, if the sunshine of Lono's presence was to come at last? But where was Lono? Perhaps in the bottom of the sea; but, if alive, she resolved to find him, even though the search took her through all the group to the barren rocks of Kaula.

Rounding the capes of Kau and sailing nearly northward, Kaikilani first stopped at Lahaina; but a week spent there convinced her that Lono was not on the island of Maui. The moi treated her with great respect and kindness, and offered to assist in the search for her husband on the other islands; but she declined his services, and next visited Lanai. Causing a thorough search to be made of that island, and despatching a party to the windy wastes of Kahoolawe, the queen proceeded to Molokai, to assure herself that Lono had not returned to Kalaupapa, and then set sail for Oahu. She first landed at Waikiki, on that island, but, learning that the king had established his court at Kailua, departed for that place the next day, and reached it without difficulty, for the captain of her crew was the distinguished old navigator, Kukupea, who for a wager, in the reign of Keawenui, had made the direct passage in a canoe between the Hawaiian bay of Kealakeakua and the island of Niihau without sighting intermediate land.

III.

Leaving Kaikilani entering the bay of Kailua, it will be in order to briefly refer to the adventures of Lono after his sudden departure from Kalaupapa. Half-crazed at what had occurred, to divert his thoughts from his cruelty he seized a paddle, and vigorously used it hour after hour until he was compelled to cease through exhaustion. The wind was fair, but, inspired by his example, twenty others plied the paddle ceaselessly in turns of ten, and in a few hours the royal canoe was hauled up on the beach of Kailua, on the northwestern coast of Oahu, where, as before stated, Kakuhihewa, the moi of the island, had temporarily established his court.

As Lono approached the shore his state attracted attention. A chief and priest, who had at one time been in the service of Lono's father, recognized the sail and insignia of the craft, and informed the king that it must be that some one nearly connected with the royal family of Hawaii had come to visit him. This secured to Lono a cordial and royal welcome. Houses were set apart for his accommodation, and food in abundance was provided for him and his attendants. Although he scrupulously concealed his name and rank, and in that respect enjoined the closest secrecy upon his attendants under penalty of death, his commanding presence and personal equipment rendered it apparent that he was either one of the sons of Keawenui or a chief of the highest rank below the throne.

Pleading fatigue, and courteously desiring to be left to himself until the day following, Lono partook of his evening meal, sent from the table of the king, alone and in silence, and at an early hour retired to rest. But the heat was oppressive, and thoughts of Kaikilani disturbed his slumbers, and near midnight he strolled down to his canoe on the beach to catch the cool breeze of the sea. While there another double canoe arrived from Kauai, having on board a high chiefess, who was on her way to Hawaii and had touched at Kailua for fresh water.

To pass the time Lono engaged in conversation with the fair stranger, and so interested her that she repeated to him twice a new mele that had just been composed in honor of her name—Ohaikawiliula—and which was known only to a few of the highest chiefs of Kauai. Portions of the celebrated chant are still retained by old Hawaiians.

The mele diverted his mind from bitter thoughts, and when he returned to his couch he enjoyed a refreshing sleep. At daylight the next morning the king, without disturbing his royal guest, repaired to the sea-shore for his customary bath just as the Kauai chiefess was preparing to depart. Making himself known to her, she recited to him until he was able to repeat the new mele, and then made sail for Hawaii. As she had arrived after midnight, and the mele was new, the king was pleased at the thought of being able to surprise Lono by reciting it to him; but his amazement was great and his discomfiture complete when, on meeting his guest after breakfast and bantering him to repeat the latest Kauaian mele, Lono recited in full the poem he had so quickly and correctly committed to memory the night before. This incident is related by tradition in evidence of Lono's mental capacity.

Notwithstanding the mystery which surrounded him at the court of Oahu, Lono soon became a great favorite there. No one could throw a spear so far or so accurately, and in all games and exercises of strength or skill he found no equal.

He was generous and fearless, and in his pastimes reckless of his life. Although he was beset with their smiles and blandishments, women seemed to have no charm for him, and he politely but firmly declined to avail himself of that feature of early Hawaiian hospitality which held a host to be remiss in courtesy if he failed to provide his guest with female companionship. He preferred the sturdier contests of men, and introduced to the Oahuans a number of new games of skill and muscle.

While the most of the chiefs were generous admirers of the accomplishments of their unknown visitor, a few were jealous of his popularity, among them the grand counselor of the king, Lanahuimihaku, who on one occasion sneeringly referred to him as "a nameless chief." To this taunt Lono, towering above his traducer with a menace of death in his face, replied that he would flay him alive if he ever met him beyond the protection of his king; and then he brought from his canoe the great calabash of bones, and, exhibiting the trophies of his father's prowess, chanted the names of the slain. This apprised them all that he was indeed a son of Keawenui, but which one they did not know.

But Lono's stay in Kailua was drawing to a close, for one day, while he was playing konane with the king within the enclosure of the palace grounds, Kaikilani's canoe was being drawn up on the beach below. She saw, to her great joy, the canoe of her husband, and ascertained where he might be found. Proceeding alone toward the royal mansion, with a fluttering heart she approached the enclosure, and through an opening in the wall discerned the stalwart form of Lono. Stepping aside to avoid his gaze, she began to chant his mele inoa—the song of his own name. He was startled at hearing his name mentioned in a place where he supposed it to be unknown. He raised his head and listened, and, as the words of the mele floated to him, he recognized the voice of Kaikilani. Rising to his feet, with dignity he now addressed the king:

"My royal brother, disguise is no longer necessary or fitting. I am Lonoikamakahiki, son of Keawenui and moi of Hawaii, and the gods have sent to me Kaikilani, my wife. It is her voice that we now hear."

Then, turning and approaching the wall behind which Kaikilani was standing, Lono began to chant her name, coupled with words of tenderness and reconciliation; then, springing over the obstruction, he clasped his faithful wife in his arms, and the past was forgiven and forgotten.

The rank of his guests now being known, Kakuhihewa was anxious to give them a befitting recognition; but, learning of the revolt in Hawaii and the peril of Pupuakea, Lono embarked for his kingdom at once. Reaching and passing Kohala, where he learned the rebels were in force, he landed at Kealakeakua, and immediately despatched a messenger to Pupuakea, in Kau, with information of his arrival in Puna. The brother responded promptly, and, leading his forces over a mountain path to avoid the coast villages, joined Lono at Puuanahulu. Meantime, Lono's name had brought thousands to his standard, and on the arrival of Pupuakea he boldly attacked and defeated the insurgents at Wailea. They were followed and again defeated at Kaunooa.

Reinforcements reaching the rebels from Kohala, two other battles were fought in rapid succession, both resulting in their defeat. In these engagements two of Lono's brothers were slain, and the body of one of them was offered as a sacrifice at the heiau of Puukohola.

The last of the rebels were defeated at Pololu, and the island returned to its allegiance to Lono and Kaikilani. Kanaloa-kuaana, who originated the revolt, also submitted, and was forgiven and restored to favor through the intercession of the queen.

The legends relate many subsequent romantic adventures of Lono; but he and Kaikilani both lived to good old ages, and when they died were succeeded in the sovereignty of Hawaii by lineal blood.

THE CANNIBALS OF HALEMANU

A POPULAR LEGEND OF THE SEVENTEENTH CENTURY

I.

Although barbarous to the extent to which a brave, warm-hearted and hospitable people were capable of becoming, every social, political and religious circumstance preserved by tradition tends to show that at no period of their history did the Polynesians proper—or the Hawaiian branch of the race, at least—practise cannibalism. In their migrations from the southern coasts of Asia to their final homes in the Pacific, stopping, as they did, at various groups of islands in their voluntary or compulsory journeyings, the Polynesians must have been brought in contact with cannibal tribes; but no example ever persuaded them into the habit of eating human flesh, or of regarding the appetite for it with a feeling other than that of aversion and disgust. In offering a human sacrifice it was customary for the officiating priest to remove the left eye of the victim after the lifeless body had been deposited upon the altar, and present it to the chief, who made a semblance of eating it. Even as learned and conscientious an inquirer as Judge Fornander has suggested that this custom was possibly the relic of a cannibal propensity existing among the Polynesian people far back in the past. The assumption is quite as reasonable that the rite was either a simple exhibition of bravado, or the expression of a desire on the part of the chief to thereby more strictly identify himself with the offering in the eyes of the gods.

Several traditions have come down the centuries referring to the existence of cannibal tribes or bands at one time or another in the Hawaiian archipelago, particularly on the islands of Oahu and Kauai, and harrowing stories of their exploits are a part of the folk-lore of the group. But in every instance the man-eaters are spoken of as foreigners, who came from a land unknown, maintained local footholds for brief seasons in mountain fastnesses, and in the end were either exterminated or driven from the islands by the people for their barbarous practices. It is difficult to fix, even approximately, the period of the earlier of these occurrences, as they are mentioned in connection with ruling chiefs whose names do not appear in the chronological meles surviving the destruction of the ancient priesthood. Instead of being foreigners, it is not improbable that the cannibals referred to in some of the traditions were the remnants of a race of savages found on one or more of the islands of the group when the first of the Polynesians landed there. This, it may be presumed, was somewhere near the middle of the fifth century of the Christian era.

It has generally been assumed by native historians that the ancestors of the Hawaiian people found the entire group uninhabited at the time of their arrival there. The bird, the lizard and the mouse, with an insect life confined to few varieties, were the sole occupants of that ocean paradise, with its beautiful streams, its inviting hills, its sandal forests, its cocoa and ohia groves, its flowering plains, its smiling valleys of everlasting green. But the interval between the fifth century and the eleventh—between the first and second periods of Polynesian arrival—is a broad blank in the legendary annals of Hawaii, and the absence of any record of the circumstance cannot be satisfactorily accepted as evidence that, on arriving at the group from the southern islands, the Polynesians of the fifth century did not find it sparsely occupied by an inferior and less capable people, whom they either affiliated with or destroyed. In some of the meles vague references are made to such a people, and ruins of temples are still pointed out as the work of the Menehunes—a half-mythical race or tribe, either from whom the Hawaiians descended, or with whom they were in some manner connected in the remote past.

To whatever period, however, many of these stories of cannibalism may refer, circumstances tend to show that the legends connected with the man-eaters of Halemanu are based upon events of comparatively recent centuries. The natives, who still relate fragments of these legends to those whom curiosity prompts to visit the cannibals' retreat near the northern coast of Oahu, generally refer the adventures described to the early part or middle of the eighteenth century, and a half-caste of intelligence informed the writer that his grandfather had personal knowledge of the cannibal band. Although the sharpness of the details preserved indicates that their beginning could not have been very many generations back, the occupation of Halemanu by Aikanaka and his savage followers could have occurred scarcely later than the latter part of the seventeenth century—probably during the reign of Kualii or his immediate successor, somewhere between the years 1660 and 1695. At that time Oahu was governed by a number of practically independent chiefs, whose nominal head was the governing alii-nui of the line of Kakuhihewa, of whom Kualii was the great-grandson.

It will therefore be assumed that it was near the close of the seventeenth century that Kalo Aikanaka, with two or three hundred followers, including women and children, landed at Waialua, on the northern coast of Oahu, and temporarily established himself on the sea-shore not far from that place. Ten years before, more or less, he had arrived with a considerable party at Kauai from one of the southern islands—which one tradition does not mention. The strangers came in double canoes, and, as they were in a starving condition, it was thought that they had been blown thither by adverse winds while journeying to some other islands. They were hospitably received and cared for by the people of Kauai, and for their support were given lands near the foot of the mountains back of Waimea. In complexion they were somewhat darker than the Kauaians, but otherwise did not differ greatly from them either in dress, manners, modes of living or appearance. They knew how to weave mats, construct houses of timber and thatch, make spears and knives, and hollow out canoes of all dimensions. They were familiar with the cocoanut and its uses, and required no instruction in the cultivation of kalo or taro. They were expert fishermen, and handled their weapons with dexterity. Their language, however, was entirely different from that of the Kauaians; but they soon acquired a knowledge of the latter, and in a short time could scarcely be distinguished from the natives of the island.

Although known as Kalo Aikanaka by the natives, the real name of the chief of the strangers was Kokoa. The name of his principal lieutenant or adviser, which is given as Kaaokeewe by tradition, was Lotu, or Lotua. Kokoa was of chiefly proportions, and his muscular limbs were tattooed with rude representations of birds, sharks and other fishes. His features were rather of the Papuan cast, but his hair was straight, and the expression of his face was not unpleasant. The appearance of Lotu, on the contrary, was savage and forbidding. His strength was prodigious, and he made but little disguise of his lawless instincts. The wife of Kokoa had died during the passage to Kauai, leaving with him a daughter of marriageable age named Palua. Tradition says she was very beautiful, and wore necklaces and anklets of pearls. Her eyes were bright, her teeth were white, and the ends of her braided hair touched her brown ankles as she walked. Lotu was married, but without children. He did not like them, and more than one, it is said, had been taken from the breast of Kaholekua and strangled.

The strangers brought with them two or three gods, and made others after their arrival. They knew nothing of the gods of the Kauaians, and preferred to worship their own. To this the natives did not object; but in the course of time they discovered that their tabu customs, even the most sacred, were not observed by the strangers. Their women were permitted to eat cocoanuts, bananas, and all kinds of flesh and fish, including the varieties of which native females were not allowed to partake. Fearing the wrath of the gods, the chief of the district visited Kokoa and requested him to put a stop to these pernicious practices among his people. He promised to do so, and for a time they ceased; but the offenders soon fell back into their old habit of indiscriminate eating, and the chief again visited Kokoa, prepared to put his previous request into the form of an order. The order was given, but not with the emphasis designed by the chief in making the visit, for he then met Palua for the first time, and found it difficult to speak harshly to the father of such a daughter. In fact, before he left the chief thought it well to leave the matter open for further explanation, and the next day returned to make it, and to ask

Kokoa, as well, to give him the beautiful Palua for a wife. Father and daughter both consented, and within a few days Palua accompanied the chief home as his wife. There, at least, it was expected that Palua would respect the tabus she had violated before her coming, and the chief appointed a woman to instruct her thoroughly in the regulations applicable to her changed condition. She promised everything, but secretly complied with no requirement. The chief implored her to obey the mandates of the gods, and sought to screen her acts from the eyes of others; but her misdemeanors became so flagrant that they at last came to the knowledge of the high-priest, and her life was demanded. Her husband would have returned Palua to her father, but the priest declared that her offences had been so wanton and persistent that the gods would be satisfied with nothing short of her death, and she was therefore strangled and thrown into the sea.

Learning of the death of his daughter, Kokoa in his rage slew a near kinsman of the chief and made a feast of his body, to the great delight of his followers. They were cannibals, but the fact was not known to their neighbors, as they had thus far restrained their appetites for human flesh, and avoided all mention to others of their propensity for such food. Their relish for it, however, was revived by the feast provided by the wrath of Kokoa, and they were not sorry to leave the lands they had been for some time cultivating back of Waimea, and find a home in the neighboring mountains, where they could indulge their savage tastes without restraint.

Locating in a secluded valley in the mountains of Haupu, Kokoa and his people remained there for several years. They cultivated taro and other vegetables, and for their meat depended upon such natives as they were able to capture in out-of-the-way places and drag to their ovens. Suspected of cannibalism, they were finally detected in the act of roasting a victim. Great indignation and excitement followed this discovery, and the chief of the district called for warriors to assist him in exterminating the man-eaters. But Kokoa did not wait for a hostile visit. His spies informed him of what was occurring in the valleys below, and he hastily dropped down to the opposite coast, seized a number of canoes at night, and with his followers immediately set sail for Oahu. The party first landed at Kawailoa; but a Kauaian on a visit to that place recognized one of their canoes as the property of his brother, and was about to appeal to the local chief, when they suddenly re-embarked and coasted around the island to Waialua, where they found a convenient landing and concluded to remain.

II.

We now come to the final exploits of Kokoa and his clan in Oahu. It is probable that they did not remain long in the immediate neighborhood of Waialua, where the people were numerous and unoccupied lands were scarce. Sending their scouts into the mountains in search of a safe and uninhabited retreat, one of exceptional advantages was found in the range east of Waialua, some eight or ten miles from the coast, and thither they removed. The spot selected has since been known as Halemanu. Before that time it was probably without any particular name. It is a crescent-shaped plateau of two or three hundred acres, completely surrounded by deep and almost precipitous ravines, with the exception of a narrow isthmus, scarcely wide enough for a carriage-way, connecting it with a broad area of timberless table-land stretching downward toward the sea.

Nature could scarcely have devised a place better fitted for defence, and Kokoa resolved to permanently locate there. Near the middle of the plateau he erected a temple, with stone walls two hundred feet by sixty, and twenty feet in height. This structure was also designed as a citadel, to be used in emergencies. About fifty paces from the temple was the hale of the chief—a stone building of the dimensions of perhaps fifty feet by forty. It was divided into three rooms by wicker partitions, and roofed with stout poles and thatch. Between this building and the temple was a large excavated oven, with a capacity for roasting four or five human bodies at the same time, and a few paces to the westward was the great carving-platter of Kokoa. This was a slightly basin-shaped stone rising a foot or more above the surface, and having a superfice of perhaps six by four feet. A little hewing here and there transformed it into a convenient carving-table, from which hundreds of human bodies were apportioned to his followers by Kokoa, who reserved for himself the hearts and livers, as delicacies to which his rank entitled him. The lines of the buildings described may still be traced among the tall grass, and the oily-appearing surface of the carving-table, known as "Kalo's ipukai" bears testimony to this day to the use made of it by the cannibals of Halemanu. The platter is now almost level with the surface of the ground, and its rim has been chipped down by relic-hunters, but time and the spoliations of the curious have not materially changed its shape.

Having provided the plateau with these conveniences and the huts necessary to accommodate his people, Kokoa next put the place in a condition for defence by cutting the tops of the exposed slopes leading to it into perpendicular declivities, and erecting a strong building covering the width and almost entire length of the narrow back-bone connecting it with the plain below. There was then no means of reaching the plateau except by a path zigzagging down the upper side to the timbered gulches beyond, or by the trail passing directly through the building occupying the apex of the isthmus.

Of this entrance Lotu, the savage lieutenant of Kokoa, was made the custodian. And there he sat in all weather, watching for passers, the most of whom, if acceptable, he found a pretext for slaying and sending to the great oven of his companions. His almost sleepless watchfulness was due less to a disposition to serve others than to his merciless instincts, which found gratification in blood-letting and torture. Tradition says there was a hideous humor in the manner in which he dealt with many of his victims. In allowing them to pass he inquired the objects of their visits either to the plateau or the gulches beyond. They informed him, perhaps, that they were in quest of hala leaves, of poles for huts, of wood for surf-boards, of small trees for spears, or of flints for cutting implements, as the case may have been. When they returned he examined their burdens closely, and if aught was found beyond the thing of which they were specifically in search—even though so trifling an object as a walking-staff, or a twig or flower gathered by the way—he denounced them as thieves and liars, and slew them on the spot.

In this manner many hundreds of people were slain and eaten; but as no one ever returned to tell the story of what was transpiring at Halemanu, the cannibals remained for some time undisturbed. But if their real character was not known, their isolation and strange conduct gradually gained for them the reputation of being an evil-minded and dangerous community, and visitors became so scarce at length that Lotu found it necessary to drop down into the valleys occasionally in search of victims. Nor were these expeditions, which demanded great caution, always successful; and when they failed, Lotu sometimes secretly killed and sent to the oven one of his own people, with faces mutilated beyond recognition. Among these were all of his own relatives and two of the three brothers of his wife. To escape the fate of the others, the surviving brother, whose name was Napopo, fled to Kauai.

In physical strength Napopo was scarcely less formidable than Lotu; but he was young in years, and lacked both skill and confidence in his powers. To supply these deficiencies, and prepare himself for a successful encounter with Lotu, which he resolved to undertake in revenge for the death of his brothers, he sought the most expert wrestlers and boxers on Kauai, and learned from them the secrets of their prowess. He trained himself in running, swimming, leaping, climbing, and lifting and casting great rocks, until his muscles became like hard wood, and his equal in strength and agility could with difficulty be found on all the island. And he skilled himself, also, in the use of arms. He learned to catch and parry flying spears, and hurl them with incredible force and precision. From the sling he could throw a stone larger than a cocoanut, and the battle-axe he readily wielded with one hand few men were able to swing with two. Having thus accomplished himself, and still distrustful of his powers, he made the offer of a canoe nine paces in length to any one who in a trial should prove to be his master either in feats of strength or the handling of warlike weapons. Many contested for the prize, but Napopo found a superior in no one.

During the contests a strong man, with large jaws and

a thick neck, came forward and challenged Napopo to compete with him in lifting heavy burdens with the teeth. The bystanders were amused at the proposal, and Napopo was compelled by their remarks and laughter to accept it, although he regarded it as frivolous. Fastening around his middle a girdle of cords, he cast himself on the ground and said to the man: "Now with your teeth lift me to the level of your breast." Stooping and seizing the girdle in his teeth, the man with a great effort lifted Napopo to the height demanded. The other was then girded in the same manner. He seemed to be confident of victory, and said to Napopo, as he threw himself at his feet: "You will do well if you raise me to the level of your knees." Napopo made no reply, but bent and gathered the girdle well between his teeth, and raised the body to the height of his loins. "Higher!" exclaimed the man, thinking the strength of his antagonist was even then taxed to its utmost; "my body is scarcely free from the ground!" He had scarcely uttered these words before Napopo rose erect, and with a quick motion threw him completely over his head. Bruised and half-stunned by the fall, the man struggled to his feet, and, with a look of wonder at Napopo, hurriedly left the place to escape the jeers of the shouting witnesses of his defeat.

Now confident of his strength and satisfied with his skill, Napopo returned to Oahu in the canoe which so many had failed to win. Landing at Waialua, he by some means learned that his sister, Kaholekua, the wife of Lotu, had been killed by her husband. Arming himself with a spear and knife of sharks' teeth, Napopo proceeded to Halemanu. Arriving at the house barring the entrance to the stronghold, he was met at the door by Lotu. Their recognition was cold. The eyes of Lotu gleamed with satisfaction. No longer intimidated, as in the past,

Napopo paid back the look with a bearing of defiance.

"Leave your spear and enter," said Lotu, curtly.

Napopo leaned his spear against the house and stepped within, observing, as he did so, that Lotu in his movements kept within reach of an axe and javelin lying near the door.

"Where is Kaholekua?" inquired Napopo.

"There," replied Lotu, sullenly, pointing toward a curtain of mats stretched across a corner of the room.

Without a word Napopo stepped to the curtain and drew it aside. He expected to find his sister dead, if at all, but she was still living, although lying insensible from wounds which seemed to be mortal. With a heart swelling with rage and anguish, he closed the curtain and returned to the door. He could not trust himself to speak, and therefore silently stepped without, in the hope that Lotu would leave his weapons and follow him. To this end he stood for a few minutes near the entrance, as if overwhelmed with grief, when Lotu cautiously approached the door. Advancing a step farther, Napopo suddenly turned and seized him before he could reach his weapons, and a desperate bare-handed struggle followed. Both were giants, and the conflict was ferocious and deadly. From one side to the other of the narrow isthmus they battled, biting, tearing, pulling, breaking, with no decided advantage to either; but the endurance of Napopo was greater than that of his older antagonist, and in the end he was able to inflict injury without receiving dangerous punishment in return. Both of them were covered with blood, and their maros had been rent away in the struggle, leaving them perfectly nude.

Although Napopo had in a measure overpowered his mighty adversary, he found it difficult to kill him with his naked hands. He could tear and disfigure his flesh, but was unable to strangle him or break his spine. He therefore re-solved to drag him to the verge of the precipice, and hurl him over it into the rocky abyss below. Struggling and fighting, the edge of the gulf was reached, when Lotu suddenly fastened his arms around his antagonist, and with a howl of desperation plunged over the brink. Dropping downward to destruction together, Lotu's head was caught in the fork of a tree near the bottom of the declivity and torn from the body, and Napopo, clasped in the embrace of the lifeless but rigid trunk, fell dead and mangled among the rocks of the ravine still farther down.

Recovering her consciousness during the battle, Kahol-ekua dragged herself from the house just in time to witness the descent of the desperate combatants over the precipice. Approaching the verge, she uttered a feeble wail of anguish and plunged headlong down the declivity, her mangled re-mains lodging within a few paces of those of her husband and brother.

The conclusion of these tragical scenes was observed by a party from the plateau above—one tradition says by Kokoa himself. However this may be, the cannibal chief concluded that Halemanu was no longer a desirable retreat, and a few days after crossed the mountains to Waianae with his remain-ing followers, and soon thereafter set sail with them for other lands. What became of the party is not known; but with their departure ends the latest and most vivid of the several legends of cannibalism in the Hawaiian archipelago.

KAALA, THE FLOWER
OF LANAI

A STORY OF THE SPOUTING
CAVE OF PALIKAHOLO

I.

Beneath one of the boldest of the rocky bluffs against which dash the breakers of Kaumalapau Bay, on the little island of Lanai, is the Puhio-Kaala, or "Spouting Cave of Kaala." The only entrance to it is through the vortex of a whirlpool, which marks the place where, at intervals, the receding waters rise in a column of foam above the surface. Within, the floor of the cave gradually rises from the opening beneath the waters until a landing is reached above the level of the tides, and to the right and left, farther than the eye can penetrate by the dim light struggling through the surging waves, stretch dank and shelly shores, where crabs, polypii, sting-rays and other noisome creatures of the deep find protection against their larger enemies.

This cavern was once a favorite resort of Mooalii, the great lizard-god; but as the emissaries of Ukanipo, the shark-god, annoyed him greatly and threatened to imprison him within it by piling a mountain of rocks against the opening, he abandoned it and found a home in a cave near Kaulapapa, in the neighboring island of Molokai, where many rude temples were erected to him by the fishermen.

Before the days of Kamehameha I. resolute divers frequently visited the Spouting Cave, and on one occasion fire, enclosed in a small calabash, was taken down through the whirlpool, with the view of making a light and exploring its mysterious chambers; but the fire was scattered and extinguished by an unseen hand, and those who brought it hastily retreated to escape a shower of rocks sent down upon them from the roof of the cavern. The existence of the cave is still known, and the whirlpool and spouting column marking the entrance to it are pointed out; but longer and longer have grown the intervals between the visits of divers to its sunless depths, until the present generation can point to not more than one, perhaps, who has ventured to enter them.

Tradition has brought down the outlines of a number of supernatural and romantic stories connected with the Spouting Cave, but the nearest complete and most recent of these mookaaos is the legend of Kaala, the flower of Lanai, which is here given at considerably less length than native narration accords it.

It was during an interval of comparative quiet, if not of peace, in the stormy career of Kamehameha I., near the close of the last century, and after the battle of Maunalei, that he went with his court to the island of Lanai for a brief season of recreation. The visit was not made for the purpose of worshipping at the great heiau of Kaunola, which was then half in ruins, or at any of the lesser temples scattered here and there over the little island, and dedicated, in most instances, to fish-gods. He went to Kealia simply to enjoy a few days of rest away from the scenes of his many conflicts, and feast for a time upon the affluent fishing-grounds of that locality.

He made the journey with six double canoes, all striped with yellow, and his own bearing the royal ensign. He took with him his war-god, Kaili, and a small army of attendants, consisting of priests, kahunas, kahili and spittoon-bearers, stewards, cooks and other household servants, as well as a retinue of distinguished chiefs with their personal retainers in their own canoes, and a hundred warriors in the capacity of a royal guard.

Landing, the victorious chief was received with enthusiasm by the five or six thousand people then inhabiting the island. He took up his residence in the largest of the several cottages provided for him and his personal attendants. Provisions were brought in abundance, and flowers and sweet-scented herbs and vines were contributed without stint. The chief and his titled attendants were garlanded with them. They were strewn in his path, cast at his door and thrown upon his dwelling, until their fragrance seemed to fill all the air.

Among the many who brought offerings of flowers was the beautiful Kaala, "the sweet-scented flower of Lanai," as she was called. She was a girl of fifteen, and in grace and beauty had no peer on the island. She was the daughter of Oponui, a chief of one of the lower grades, and her admirers were counted by the hundreds. Of the many who sought her as a wife was Mailou, "the bone-breaker." He was a huge, muscular savage, capable of crushing almost any ordinary man in an angry embrace; and while Kaala hated, feared and took every occasion to avoid him, her father favored his suit, doubtless pleased at the thought of securing in a son-in-law a friend and champion so distinguished for his strength and ferocity.

As Kaala scattered flowers before the chief her graceful movements and modesty were noted by Kaaialii, and when he saw her face he was enraptured with its beauty. Although young in years, he was one of Kamehameha's most valued lieutenants, and had distinguished himself in many battles. He was of chiefly blood and bearing, with sinewy limbs and a handsome face, and when he stopped to look into the eyes of Kaala and tell her that she was beautiful, she thought the words, although they had been frequently spoken to her by others, had never sounded so sweetly to her before. He asked her for a simple flower, and she twined a lei for his neck. He asked her for a smile, and she looked up into his face and gave him her heart.

They saw each other the next day, and the next, and then Kaaialii went to his chief and said: "I love the beautiful Kaala, daughter of Oponui. Your will is law. Give her to me for a wife."

For a moment Kamehameha smiled without speaking, and then replied: "The girl is not mine to give. We must be just. I will send for her father. Come tomorrow."

Kaaialii had hoped for a different answer; but neither protest nor further explanation was admissible, and all he could do was to thank the king and retire.

A messenger brought Oponui to the presence of Kamehameha. He was received kindly, and told that Kaaialii loved Kaala and desired to make her his wife. The information kindled the wrath of Oponui. He hated Kaaialii, but did not dare to exhibit his animosity before the king. He was in the battle of Maunalei, where he narrowly escaped death at the hands of Kaaialii, after his spear had found the heart of one of his dearest friends, and he felt that he would rather give his daughter to the sharks than to one who had sought his life and slain his friend. But he pretended to regard the proposal with favor, and, in answer to the king, expressed regret that he had promised his daughter to Mailou, the bone-breaker. "However," he continued, "in respect to the interest which it has pleased you, great chief, to take in the matter, I am content that the girl shall fall to the victor in a contest with bare hands between Mailou and Kaaialii."

The proposal seemed to be fair, and, not doubting that Kaaialii would promptly accept it, the king gave it his approval, and the contest was fixed for the day following. Oponui received the announcement with satisfaction, not doubting that Mailou would crush Kaaialii in his rugged embrace as easily as he had broken the bones of many an adversary.

News of the coming contest spread rapidly, and the next day thousands of persons assembled at Kealia to witness it. Kaala was in an agony of fear. The thought of becoming the wife of the bone-breaker almost distracted her, for it was said that he had had many wives, all of whom had disappeared one after another as he tired of them, and the whisper was that he had crushed and thrown them into the sea. And, besides, she loved Kaaialii, and deemed it scarcely possible that he should be able to meet and successfully combat the prodigious strength and ferocity of one who had never been subdued.

As Kaaialii was approaching the spot where the contest was to take place, in the presence of Kamehameha and his court and a large concourse of less distinguished spectators, Kaala sprang from the side of her father, and, seizing the young chief by the hand, exclaimed:

"You have indeed slain my people in war, but rescue me from the horrible embrace of the bone-breaker, and I will catch the squid and beat the kapa for you all my days!"

With a dark frown upon his face, Oponui tore the girl

from her lover before he could reply. Kaaialii followed her with his eyes until she disappeared among the spectators, and then pressed forward through the crowd and stepped within the circle reserved for the combatants. Mailou was already there. He was indeed a muscular brute, with long arms, broad shoulders and mighty limbs tattooed with figures of sharks and birds of prey. He was naked to the loins, and, as Kaaialii approached, his fingers opened and closed, as if impatient to clutch and tear his adversary in pieces.

Although less bulky than the bone-breaker, Kaaialii was large and perfectly proportioned, with well-knit muscles and loins and shoulders suggestive of unusual strength. Nude, with the exception of a maro, he was a splendid specimen of vigorous manhood; but, in comparison with those of the bone-breaker, his limbs appeared to be frail and feminine, and a general expression of sympathy for the young chief was observed in the faces of the large assemblage as they turned from him to the sturdy giant he was about to encounter.

The contest was to be one of strength, courage, agility and skill combined. Blows with the clenched fist, grappling, strangling, tearing, breaking and every other injury which it was possible to inflict were permitted. In hakoko (wrestling) and moko (boxing) contests certain rules were usually observed, in order that fatal injuries might be avoided; but in the combat between Kaaialii and Mailou no rule or custom was to govern. It was to be a savage struggle to the death.

Taunt and boasting are the usual prelude to personal conflicts among the uncivilized; nor was it deemed unworthy the Saxon knight to meet his adversary with insult and bravado. The object was not more to unnerve his opponent than to steel his own courage. With the bone-breaker, however, there was little fear or doubt concerning the result. He knew the measure of his own prodigious strength, and, with a malignant smile that laid bare his shark-like teeth, he glared with satisfaction upon his rival.

"Ha! ha!" laughed the bone-breaker, taking a stride toward Kaaialii; "so you are the insane youth who has dared to meet Mailou in combat! Do you know who I am? I am the bone-breaker! In my hands the limbs of men are like tender cane. Come, and with one hand let me strangle you!"

"You will need both!" replied Kaaialii. "I know you. You are a breaker of the bones of women, not of men! You speak brave words, but have the heart of a coward. Let the word be given, and if you do not run from me to save your life, as I half-suspect you will, I will put my foot upon your broken neck before you find time to cry for mercy!"

Before Mailou could retort the word was given, and with an exclamation of rage he sprang at the throat of Kaaialii. Feigning as if to meet the shock, the latter waited until the hands of Mailou were almost at his throat, when with a quick movement he struck them up, swayed his body to the left, and with his right foot adroitly tripped his over-confident assailant. The momentum of Mailou was so great that he fell headlong to the earth. Springing upon him before he could rise, Kaaialii seized his right arm, and with a vigorous blow of the foot broke the bone below the elbow. Rising and finding his right arm useless, Mailou attempted to grapple his adversary with the left, but a well-delivered blow felled him again to the earth, and Kaaialii broke his left arm as he had broken the right. Regaining his feet, and unable to use either hand, with a wild howl of despair the bone-breaker rushed upon Kaaialii, with the view of dealing him a blow with his bent head; but the young chief again tripped him as he passed, and, seizing him by the hair as he fell, placed his knees against the back of his prostrate foe and broke his spine.

This, of course, ended the struggle, and Kaaialii was declared the victor, amidst the plaudits of the spectators and the congratulations of Kamehameha and the court. Breaking from her father, who was grievously disappointed at the un-looked-for result, and who sought to detain her, Kaala sprang through the crowd and threw herself into the arms of Kaaia-lii. Oponui would have protested, and asked that his daughter might be permitted to visit her mother before becoming the wife of Kaaialii; but the king put an end to his hopes by plac-ing the hand of Kaala in that of the victorious chief, and saying to him:

"You have won her nobly. She is now your wife. Take her with you."

Although silenced by the voice of the king, and com-pelled to submit to the conditions of a contest which he had himself proposed, Oponui's hatred of Kaaialii knew no abate-ment, and all that day and the night following he sat alone by the sea-shore, devising a means by which Kaala and her husband might be separated. He finally settled upon a plan.

The morning after her marriage Oponui visited Kaala, as if he had just returned from Mahana, where her mother was supposed to be then living. He greeted her with apparent af-fection, and was profuse in his expressions of friendship for Kaaialii. He embraced them both, and said: "I now see that you love each other; my prayer is that you may live long and happily together." He then told Kaala that Kalani, her mother, was lying dangerously ill at Mahana, and, believing that she would not recover, desired to see and bless her daughter before she died. Kaala believed the story, for her father wept when he told it, and moaned as if for the dead, and beat his breast; and, with many protestations of love, Kaaialii allowed her to depart with Oponui, with the promise from both of them that she would speedily return to the arms of her husband.

With some misgivings, Kaaialii watched her from the top of the hill above Kealia until she descended into the valley of Palawai. There leaving the path that led to Mahana, they journeyed toward the bay of Kaumalapau. Satisfied that her father was for some purpose deceiving her, Kaala protested and was about to return, when he acknowledged that her mother was not ill at Mahana, as he had represented to Kaaialii in order to secure his consent to her departure, but at the sea-shore, where she had gathered crabs, shrimps, limpets and other delicacies, and prepared a feast in celebration of her marriage.

Reassured by the plausible story, and half-disposed to pardon the deception admitted by her father, Kaala proceeded with him to the sea-shore. She saw that her mother was not there, and heard no sound but the beating of the waves against the rocks. She looked up into the face of her father for an explanation; but his eyes were cold, and a cruel smile upon his lips told her better than words that she had been betrayed.

"Where is my mother?" she inquired; and then bitterly added: "I do not see her fire by the shore. Must we search for her among the sharks?"

Oponui no longer sought to disguise his real purpose.

"Hear the truth!" he said, with a wild glare in his eyes that whitened the lips of Kaala. "The shark shall be your mate, but he will not harm you. You shall go to his home, but he will not devour you. Down among the gods of the sea I will leave you until Kaaialii, hated by me above all things that breathe, shall have left Lanai, and then I will bring you back to earth!"

Terrified at these words, Kaala screamed and sought to fly; but her heartless father seized her by the hand and dragged her along the shore until they reached a bench of the rocky bluff overlooking the opening to the Spouting Cave. Oponui was among the few who had entered the cavern through its gate of circling waters, and he did not for a moment doubt that within its gloomy walls, where he was about to place her, Kaala would remain securely hidden until such time as he might choose to restore her to the light.

Standing upon the narrow ledge above the entrance to the cave, marked by alternate whirlpool and receding column, Kaala divined the barbarous purpose of her father, and implored him to give her body to the sharks at once rather than leave her living in the damp and darkness of the Spouting Cave, to be tortured by the slimy and venomous creatures of the sea.

Deaf to her entreaties, Oponui watched until the settling column went down into the throat of the whirlpool, when he gathered the frantic and struggling girl in his arms and sprang into the circling abyss. Sinking a fathom or more below the surface, and impelled by a strong current setting toward the mouth of the cave, he soon found and was swept through the entrance, and in a few moments stood upon a rocky beach in the dim twilight of the cavern, with the half-unconscious

Kaala clinging to his neck.

The only light penetrating the cave was the little refracted through the waters, and every object that was not too dark to be seen looked greenish and ghostly. Crabs, eels, stingrays and other noisome creatures of the deep were crawling stealthily among the rocks, and the dull thunder of the battling waves was the only sound that could be distinguished.

Disengaging her arms, he placed her upon the beach above the reach of the waters, and then sat down beside her to recover his breath and wait for a retreating current to bear him to the surface. Reviving, Kaala looked around her with horror, and piteously implored her father not to leave her in that dreadful place beneath the waters.

For some time he made no reply, and then it was to tell her harshly that she might return with him if she would promise to accept the love of the chief of Olowalu, in the valley of Palawai, and allow Kaaialii to see her in the embrace of another. This she refused to do, declaring that she would perish in the cave, or the attempt to leave it, rather than be liberated on such monstrous conditions.

"Then here you will remain," said Oponui, savagely, "until I return, or the chief of Olowalu comes to bear you off to his home in Maui!" Then, rising to his feet, he continued hastily, as he noted a turn in the current at the opening: "You cannot escape without assistance. If you attempt it you will be dashed against the rocks and become the food of sharks."

With this warning Oponui turned and plunged into the water. Diving and passing with the current through the entrance, he was borne swiftly to the surface and to his full length up into the spouting column; but he coolly precipitated himself into the surrounding waters, and with a few strokes of the arms reached the shore.

II.

Kaaialii watched the departure of Kaala and her father until they disappeared in the valley of Palawai, and then gloomily returned to his hut. His fears troubled him. He thought of his beautiful Kaala, and his heart ached for her warm embrace. Then he thought of the looks and words of Oponui, and recalled in both a suggestion of deceit. Thus harassed with his thoughts, he spent the day in roaming alone among the hills, and the following night in restless slumber, with dreams of death and torture. The portentous cry of an alae roused him from his kapa-moe before daylight, and until the sun rose he sat watching the stars. Then he climbed the hill overlooking the valley of Palawai to watch for the return of Kaala, and wonder what could have detained her so long. He watched until the sun was well up in the heavens, feeling neither thirst nor hunger, and at length saw a pau fluttering in the wind far down the valley.

A woman was rapidly approaching, and his heart beat with joy, for he thought she was Kaala. Nearer and nearer she came, and Kaaialii, still hopeful, ran down to the path to meet her. Her step was light and her air graceful, and it was not until he had opened his arms to receive her that he saw that the girl was not Kaala. She was Ua, the friend of Kaala, and almost her equal in beauty. They had been reared together, and in their love for each other were like sisters. They loved the same flowers, the same wild songs of the birds, the same paths among the hills, and, now that Kaala loved Kaaialii, Ua loved him also.

Recognizing Kaaialii as she approached, Ua stopped before him, and bent her eyes to the ground without speaking.

"Where is Kaala?" inquired Kaaialii, raising the face of Ua and staring eagerly into it. "Have you seen her? Has any ill come to her? Speak!"

"I have not seen her, and know of no ill that has befallen her," replied the girl; "but I have come to tell you that Kaala has not yet reached the hut of Kalani, her mother; and as Oponui, with a dark look in his face, was seen to lead her through the forest of Kumoku, it is feared that she has been betrayed and will not be allowed to return to Kealia."

"And that, too, has been my fear since the moment I lost sight of her in the valley of Palawai," said Kaaialii. "I should not have trusted her father, for I knew him to be treacherous and unforgiving. May the wrath of the gods follow him if harm has come to her through his cruelty! But I will find her if she is on the island! The gods have given her to me, and in life or death she shall be mine!"

Terrified at the wild looks and words of Kaaialii, Ua clasped her hands in silence.

"Hark!" he continued, bending his ear toward the valley. "It seems that I hear her calling for me now!" And with an exclamation of rage and despair Kaaialii started at a swift pace down the path taken by Kaala the day before. As he hurried onward, he saw, at intervals, the footprints of Kaala in the dust, and every imprint seemed to increase his speed.

Reaching the point where the Mahana path diverged from the somewhat broader ala of the valley, he followed it for some distance hoping that Ua had been misinformed, and that Kaala had really visited her mother and might be found with her; but when he looked for and failed to find the marks of her feet where in reason they should have been seen had she gone to Mahana with her father, he returned and continued his course down the valley.

Suddenly he stopped. The footprints for which he was watching had now disappeared from the Palawai path, and for a moment he stood looking irresolutely around, as if in doubt concerning the direction next to be pursued. In his uncertainty several plans of action presented themselves. One was, to see what information could be gathered from Kaala's mother at Mahana, another to follow the Palawai valley to the sea, and a third to return to Kealia and consult a kaula. While these various suggestions were being rapidly canvassed, and before any conclusion could be reached, the figure of a man was seen approaching from the valley below.

Kaaialii secreted himself behind a rock, where he could watch the path without being seen. The man drew nearer and nearer, until at last Kaaialii was enabled to distinguish the features of Oponui, of all men the one whom he most desired to meet. His muscles grew rigid with wrath, and his hot breath burned the rock behind which he was crouching. He buried his fingers in the earth to teach them patience, and clenched his teeth to keep down a struggling exclamation of vengeance. And so he waited until Oponui reached a curve in the path which brought him, in passing, within a few paces of the eyes that were savagely glaring upon him, and the next moment the two men stood facing each other.

Startled at the unexpected appearance of Kaaialii,

Oponui betrayed his guilt at once by attempting to fly; but, with the cry of "Give me Kaala!" Kaaialii sprang forward and endeavored to seize him by the throat.

A momentary struggle followed; but Oponui was scarcely less powerful than his adversary, and, his shoulders being bare, he succeeded in breaking from the grasp of Kaaialii and seeking safety in flight toward Kealia.

With a cry of disappointment, Kaaialii started in pursuit. Both were swift of foot, and the race was like that of a hungry shark following his prey. One was inspired by fear and the other with rage, and every muscle of the runners was strained. Leaving the valley path, Oponui struck for Kealia by a shorter course across the hills. He hoped the roughness of the route and his better knowledge of it would give him an advantage; but Kaaialii kept closely at his heels. On they sped, up and down hills, across ravines and along rocky ridges, until they reached Kealia, when Oponui suddenly turned to the left and made a dash for the temple and puhonua not far distant. Kaaialii divined his purpose, and with a last supreme effort sought to thwart it. Gaining ground with every step, he made a desperate grasp at the shoulder of Oponui just as the latter sprang through the entrance and dropped to the earth exhausted within the protecting walls of the puhonua. Kaaialii attempted to follow, but two priests promptly stepped into the portal and refused to allow him to pass.

"Stand out of the way, or I will strangle you both!" exclaimed Kaaialii, fiercely, as he threw himself against the guards.

"Are you insane?" said another long-haired priest, stepping forward with a tabu staff in his hand. "Do you not know that this is a puhonua, sacred to all who seek its protection? Would you bring down upon yourself the wrath of the gods by shedding blood within its walls?"

"If I may not enter, then drive him forth!" replied Kaaia-lii, pointing toward Oponui, who was lying upon the ground a few paces within, intently regarding the proceedings at the gate.

"That cannot be," returned the priest. "Should he will to leave, the way will not be closed to him; otherwise he may remain in safety."

"Coward!" cried Kaaialii, addressing Oponui in a taunt-ing tone. "Is it thus that you seek protection from the anger of an unarmed man? A pau would better become you than a maro. You should twine leis and beat kapa with women, and think no more of the business of men. Come without the walls, if your trembling limbs will bear you, and I will serve you as I did your friend, the breaker of women's bones. Come, and I will tear from your throat the tongue that lied to Kaala, and feed it to the dogs!"

A malignant smile wrinkled the face of Oponui, as he thought of Kaala in her hiding-place under the sea, but he made no reply.

"Do you fear me?" continued Kaaialii. "Then arm your-self with spear and battle-axe, and with bare hands I will meet and strangle you!"

Oponui remained silent, and in a paroxysm of rage and disappointment Kaaialii threw himself upon the ground and cursed the tabu that barred him from his enemy.

His friends found and bore him to his hut, and Ua, with gentle arts and loving hands, sought to soothe and comfort him. But he would not be consoled. He talked and thought alone of Kaala, and, hastily partaking of food that he might retain his strength, started again in search of her. Pitying his distress, Ua followed him—not closely, but so that she might not lose sight of him altogether.

He traveled in every direction, stopping neither for food nor rest. Of every one he met he inquired for Kaala, and called her name in the deep valleys and on the hill-tops. Wandering near the sacred spring at the head of the waters of Kealia, he met a white-haired priest bearing from the fountain a calabash of water for ceremonial use in one of the temples. The priest knew and feared him, for his looks were wild, and humbly offered him water.

"I ask not for food or water, old man," said Kaaialii. "You are a priest—perhaps a kaula. Tell me where I can find Kaala, the daughter of Oponui, and I will pile your altars with sacrifices!"

"Son of the long spear," replied the priest, "I know you seek the sweet-smelling flower of Palawai. Her father alone knows of her hiding-place. But it is not here in the hills, nor is it in the valleys. Oponui loves and frequents the sea. He hunts for the squid in dark places, and dives for the great fish in deep waters. He knows of cliffs that are hollow, and of caves with entrances below the waves. He goes alone to the rocky shore, and sleeps with the fish-gods, who are his friends. He—"

"No more of him!" interrupted the chief, impatiently. "Tell me what has become of Kaala!"

"Be patient, and you shall hear," resumed the priest. "In one of the caverns of the sea, known to Oponui and others, has Kaala been hidden. So I see her now. The place is dark and her heart is full of terror. Hasten to her. Be vigilant, and you will find her; but sleep not, or she will be the food of the creatures of the sea."

Thanking the priest, Kaaialii started toward the bay of Kaumalapau, followed by the faithful Ua, and did not rest until he stood upon the bluff of Palikaholo, overlooking the sea. Wildly the waves beat against the rocks. Looking around, he could discern no hiding-place along the shore, and the thunder of the breakers and the screams of the sea-gulls were the only sounds to be heard. In despair he raised his voice and wildly exclaimed:

"Kaala! O Kaala! where are you? Do you sleep with the fish-gods, and must I seek you in their homes among the sunken shores?"

The bluff where he was standing overlooked and was immediately above the Spouting Cave, from the submerged entrance to which a column of water was rising above the surface and breaking into spray. In the mist of the upheaval he thought he saw the shadowy face and form of Kaala, and in the tumult of the rushing waters fancied that he heard her voice calling him to come to her.

"Kaala, I come!" he exclaimed, and with a wild leap sprang from the cliff to clasp the misty form of his bride.

He sank below the surface, and, as the column disappeared with him and he returned no more, Ua wailed upon the winds a requiem of love and grief in words like these:

> "Oh! dead is Kaaialii, the young chief of Hawaii,
> The chief of few years and many battles!
> His limbs were strong and his heart was gentle;

His face was like the sun, and he was without fear.
Dead is the slayer of the bone-breaker;
Dead is the chief who crushed the bones of Mailou;
Dead is the lover of Kaala and the loved of Ua.
For his love he plunged into the deep waters;
For his love he gave his life. Who is like Kaaialii?
Kaala is hidden away, and I am lonely;
Kaaialii is dead, and the black kapa is over my
heart:
Now let the gods take the life of Ua!"

With a last look at the spot where Kaaialii had disappeared, Ua hastened to Kealia, and at the feet of Kamehameha told of the rash act of the despairing husband of Kaala. The king was greatly grieved at the story of Ua, for he loved the young chief almost as if he had been his son. "It is useless to search for the body of Kaaialii," he said, "for the sharks have eaten it." Then, turning to one of his chiefs, he continued: "No pile can be raised over his bones. Send for Ualua, the poet, that a chant may be made in praise of Kaaialii."

Approaching nearer, Papakua, a priest, requested permission to speak. It was granted, and he said:

"Let me hope that my words may be of comfort. I have heard the story of Ua, and cannot believe that the young chief is dead. The spouting waters into which Kaaialii leaped mark the entrance to the cave of Palikaholo. Following downward the current, has he not been drawn into the cavern, where he has found Kaala, and may still be living? Such, at least, is my thought, great chief."

"A wild thought, indeed!" replied the king; "yet there is

some comfort in it, and we will see how much of truth it may reveal."

Preparations were hastily made, and with four of his sturdiest oarsmen Kamehameha started around the shore for the Spouting Cave under the bluff of Palikaholo, preceded by Ua in a canoe with Keawe, her brother.

III.

When Kaaialii plunged into the sea he had little thought of anything but death. Grasping at the spouting column as he descended, it seemed to sink with him to the surface, and even below it, and in a moment he felt himself being propelled downward and toward the cliff by a strong current. Reckless-ly yielding to the action of the waters, he soon discerned an opening in the submerged base of the bluff, and without an effort was drawn swiftly into it. The force of the current sub-sided, and to his surprise his head rose above the surface and he was able to breathe. His feet touched a rocky bottom, and he rose and looked around with a feeling of bewilderment. His first thought was that he was dead and had reached the dark shores of Po, where Milu, prince of death, sits enthroned in a grove of kou trees; but he smote his breast, and by the smart knew that he was living, and had been borne by the waters into a cave beneath the cliff from which he had leaped to grasp the misty form of Kaala.

Emerging from the water, Kaaialii found himself stand-ing on the shore of a dimly-lighted cavern. The air was chilly, and slimy objects touched his feet, and others fell splashing into the water from the rocks. He wondered whether it would be possible for him to escape from the gloomy place, and began to watch the movements of the waters near the opening, when a low moan reached his ear.

It was the voice of Kaala. She was lying near him in the darkness on the slimy shore. Her limbs were bruised and lacerated with her fruitless attempts to leave the cave, and she no longer possessed the strength to repel the crabs and other loathsome creatures that were drinking her blood and feeding upon her quivering flesh.

"It is the wailing of the wind, or perhaps of some demon of the sea who makes this horrible place his home," thought Kaaialii.

He feared neither death nor its ministers; yet something like a shudder possessed him as he held his breath and listened, but he heard nothing but the thunder of the breakers against the cavern walls.

"Who speaks?" he exclaimed, advancing a pace or two back into the darkness.

A feeble moan, almost at his feet, was the response.

Stooping and peering intently before him, he distinguished what seemed to be the outlines of a human form. Approaching and bending over it, he caught the murmur of his own name.

"It is Kaala! Kaaialii is here!" he cried, as he tenderly folded her in his arms and bore her toward the opening. Seating himself in the dim light, he pushed back the hair from her cold face, and sought to revive her with caresses and words of endearment. She opened her eyes, and, nestling closer to his breast, whispered to the ear that was bent to her lips:

"I am dying, but I am happy, for you are here."

He sought to encourage her. He told her that he had come to save her; that the gods, who loved her and would not let her die, had told him where to find her; that he would take her to his home in Kohala, and always love her as he loved her then.

She made no response. There was a sad smile upon her cold lips. He placed his hand upon her heart, and found that it had ceased to beat. She was dead, but he still held the precious burden in his arms; and hour after hour he sat there on the gloomy shore of the cavern, seeing only the pallid face of Kaala, and feeling only that he was desolate.

At length he was aroused by the splashing of water within the cave. He looked up, and Ua, the gentle and unselfish friend of Kaala, stood before him, followed a moment after by Kamehameha. The method of entering and leaving the cave was known to Keawe, and he imparted the information to his sister. Ua first leaped into the whirlpool, and the dauntless Kamehameha did not hesitate in following.

As the king approached, Kaaialii rose to his feet and stood sadly before him. He uttered no word, but with bent head pointed to the body of Kaala.

"I see," said the king, softly; "the poor girl is dead. She could have no better burial-place. Come, Kaaialii, let us leave it."

Kaaialii did not move. It was the first time that he had ever hesitated in obeying the orders of his chief.

"What! would you remain here?" said the king. "Would you throw your life away for a girl? There are others as fair. Here is Ua; she shall be your wife, and I will give you the valley of Palawai. Come, let us leave here at once, lest some angry god close the entrance against us!"

"Great chief," replied Kaaialii, "you have always been kind and generous to me, and never more so than now. But hear me. My life and strength are gone. Kaala was my life, and she is dead. How can I live without her? You are my chief. You have asked me to leave this place and live. It is the first request of yours that I have ever disobeyed. It shall be the last!"

Then seizing a stone, with a swift, strong blow he crushed in brow and brain, and fell dead upon the body of Kaala.

A wail of anguish went up from Ua. Kamehameha spoke not, moved not. Long he gazed upon the bodies before him; and his eye was moist and his strong lip quivered as, turning away at last, he said: "He loved her indeed!"

Wrapped in kapa, the bodies were laid side by side and left in the cavern; and there to-day may be seen the bones of Kaala, the flower of Lanai, and of Kaaialii, her knightly lover, by such as dare to seek the passage to them through the whirlpool of Palikaholo.

Meles of the story of the tragedy were composed and chanted before Kamehameha and his court at Kealia, and since then the cavern has been known as Puhio-kaala, or "Spouting Cave of Kaala."

THE DESTRUCTION OF THE TEMPLES

THE LAST GREAT DEFENDER OF THE HAWAIIAN GODS

I.

On the 1st of October, 1819, a fleet of four canoes bearing the royal colors set sail from Kawaihae, in the district of Kohala, on the northwestern coast of Hawaii. The canoes were large and commodious, and were occupied by between sixty and seventy persons, a portion of whom were females. The most of the men were large, muscular and over six feet in height, while the dress and bearing of many of the women indicated that they were of the tabu and chiefly classes.

The costumes of a number of those of both sexes who seemed to be of rank were a strange admixture of native and foreign fabric and fashion. American and European manufactures were beginning to find a market in the islands, and the persons of many were adorned with rich cloths, jewelry and other tokens of civilization. Their weapons and utensils were largely of metal, and a squad of ten warriors armed with muskets, in one of the canoes, showed that the white man's methods of warfare had received the early and earnest attention of the Hawaiian chiefs and leaders.

The canoe leading the little squadron was double, with covered apartments extending into and across the united decks of both, and the persons occupying it, with the exception of soldiers, sailors and servants, were distinguished alike for their gaudy trappings and a boisterous merriment infusing a feeling of jollity throughout the fleet. In this canoe was Liholiho, who, on the death of his distinguished father, Kamehameha I., something less than five months before, had become sole monarch of the Hawaiian group. In addition to two of his queens, he was accompanied by Kapihe, the commander of the royal vessels; Kekuanaoa, the royal treasurer, and a retinue of chiefly friends and personal attendants.

On the 8th of the previous May his royal father had died at Kailua, leaving to Liholiho the kingdom his arms had won, with Kaahumanu as second in authority and guardian of the realm. The morning following the death of his father Liholiho left Kailua for Kohala to avoid defilement, and there remained for ten days, when he returned to Kailua and formally assumed the sceptre. At the end of the season of mourning, for superstitious reasons the young king again left for Kohala, and took up his residence for a time at Kawaihae. Remaining there until the 1st of October, on the advice of Kaahumanu he had started on his return to Kailua.

During the brief residence of Liholiho at Kawaihae, Kaahumanu inaugurated a vigorous conspiracy against the priesthood, and resolved to persuade the young king to repudiate the religion and tabus of his fathers. In this scheme she was assisted by Keopuolani, the mother of Liholiho; Kalaimoku, the prime minister, and Hewahewa, the high-priest, who claimed descent from the renowned Paao.

In the latter part of the reign of the first Kamehameha the gods and tabus of the priesthood began to lose something of their sanctity in the estimation of the masses. Although the first Christian missionaries to the islands did not arrive until nearly a year after the death of Kamehameha I., many trading and war vessels had touched at Hawaiian ports during the two preceding decades. No very clear idea of the Christian religion had been imparted to the natives by the sailors and traders with whom they had been brought in contact; but it could not have escaped their observation that the foreigner's disregard of the tabu brought with it no punishment, and they very naturally began to question the divinity of a religious code limited in its scope to the Hawaiian people.

The results of this growing scepticism were frequent violations of the tabu. To check this seditious tendency summary punishments were inflicted. A woman was put to death for entering the eating apartment of her husband, and Jarvis relates that three men were sacrificed at Kealakeakua, a short time before the death of Kamehameha—one of them for putting on the maro of a chief, another for eating a forbidden article, and the third for leaving a house that was tabu and entering one that was not. Kamehameha had learned something of the religion of the foreigners, but not enough to impress him greatly in its favor; and when questioned concerning it during his last illness he replied that he should die in the faith of his fathers, although he thought it well that his successor should give the subject attention.

Different motives influenced the leaders in this conspiracy against the religion and tabus of the group. Kaahumanu, the favorite wife of Kamehameha I., but the mother of none of his children, was bold, ambitious and unscrupulous. Left second in authority under the young king, she chafed at the restraints imposed by the tabu upon her sex. Many of the most palatable foods were denied her by custom, and in her intercourse with foreigners acts of courtesy were chilled and hampered by numerous and irksome tabu interdictions. To enable her to eat and drink of whatever her appetites craved, and to do so in the presence of males, Kaahumanu was prepared to strike at the roots of a religious system which had maintained her ancestors in place and power, even though she had no definite knowledge of the new faith with which she hoped to supplant it.

Although the uncle of one of the wives of Liholiho—Kekauonohi— Kalaimoku was not of distinguished rank. He was a chief of decided ability, however, and had been by degrees advanced under the first Kamehameha, until he became the prime minister of the second. Not being a tabu chief by birth, he was easily persuaded by Kaahumanu to lend his assistance in depriving those of higher rank of their tabu prerogatives, and to this end he and his brother Boki were baptized by the Roman Catholic chaplain of the French corvette L'Uranie shortly after the assumption of the government by Liholiho. This was done while the young king was residing at Kawaihae, and without his knowledge.

Keopuolani, the political wife of Kamehameha I., and the mother of Liholiho, Kauikeaouli and Nahienaena, was the daughter of Kiwalao, and of supreme tabu rank. So well was this recognized that her distinguished husband, it is related, always approached her with his face to the earth. She lacked decision of character, however, and her adhesion to the conspiracy against the tabu was doubtless due to the influence over her of the crafty Kaahumanu.

Whatever may have been the motives of others, the apostasy of Hewahewa seems to have been the result of conviction. Being the high-priest of Hawaii, he had everything to lose and nothing to profit by the destruction of the religious system of which he was the supreme and honored head. Of an inquiring mind, the little knowledge he had gained of the new creed had convinced him of the inconsistency of his own, and when the time came to strike he acted boldly. His hand was the first to apply the torch to the temples. Had he hesitated the conspiracy would have failed, for the influence of the high-priest with the masses at that time was second only to that of the king.

Liholiho was strong only in his attachments. Born in 1797, when the group had been consolidated under one government and further wars were not apprehended, he had not been given that austere and solid training in civil and military life imparted to the princes of the previous generation. He was attracted by the vices rather than the virtues of the foreigners at intervals visiting the islands, and, realizing that his future was secure, had devoted almost exclusively to pleasure the ripening years of his youth. Light-hearted, affectionate and gentle, he had shown so little taste for public affairs at the age of twenty-two that his dying father, in bequeathing to him the sceptre, deemed it prudent to accompany it with the condition that, should he wield it unworthily, the supreme power should devolve upon Kaahumanu.

These were the prominent actors in the scheme for the destruction of the priesthood, and this the character of the young king who had been tarrying for some months at Kawaihae, and to whom a message had been sent by Kaahumanu, informing him that, on his return to Kailua, she would openly set the gods at defiance and declare against the tabu. This information did not greatly astonish Liholiho. He knew of the growing hostility to the tabu; had talked with Hewahewa on the subject; had learned that his mother had failed to respect it on late occasions, and had himself seen it violated without harm to the offender. Yet he feared the consequences of an open declaration against the priesthood.

He remembered the fate of Hua, whose bones whitened in the sun. He knew that his arrival at Kailua would precipitate the crisis, and compel him either to renounce or defend the gods of his fathers; and after leaving Kawaihae, as we have seen, with a party occupying four canoes, he pursued his way very leisurely toward Kailua, seemingly in no haste to reach his destination.

Moving southward, and passing the rocky point immediately north of Puako, sail was shortened in the royal fleet, and the canoes drifted slowly along the coast, taking just wind enough to hold their course. Carousings were heard in the royal quarters. Liholiho appeared, and, waving his hand to a group of men and women forward, a wild hula dance was soon in progress, to the accompaniment of drums and rattling calabashes. The king watched the dancers for some time with a vacant air, and then began to mark the drum-beats with his feet. The emphasis of the movement increased, until, dismissing his dignity, his voice finally rose above the rude music, and he began to dance with an enthusiasm which seemed to be almost frenzied. Others of the royal party joined in the revelry, and for half an hour or more the vessel was the scene of tumultuous merriment. Bottles and calabashes of intoxicating liquors were then passed from one to another of the companions of the king, and the hula was continued, followed by chants, meles and other methods of enjoyment. Drinking was frequent, and the humbler members of the party were sparingly supplied with gin, whiskey and other stimulants. Similar scenes were transpiring in the canoes following, and the debauch was the wildest ever witnessed on any one of the eight Hawaiian seas.

"Let us make drunk the water-gods!" exclaimed the king.

"Here, Kuula, is a taste for you; and here, Ukanipo, is your share!" And he tossed into the ocean two bottles of liquor.

"Let us hope the gods may not be angered by the unusual sacrifice," said Laanui, one of the favorite companions of the king. He spoke seriously, and Liholiho's face wore a troubled expression for a moment as he replied:

"Then you have not yet lost faith in the gods, Laanui?"

"No," was the prompt answer of Laanui.

The king did not continue the conversation. Turning and beckoning to a servant, more liquor was brought, after which the revelry was continued all through the day and far into the night. Meanwhile, so little progress had been made that at noon the next day the fleet was off Kiholo.

For another twenty-four hours the feasting, drinking and dancing continued, when the revelers were met by a double canoe sent by Kaahumanu from Kailua in search of the royal party. The messengers of his chief counselor were courteously received by Liholiho, and, hoisting all sail, he was escorted by them to Kailua, where he was warmly welcomed by Kaahumanu and the members of the royal family.

Appearances of dissipation were plainly visible in the language and bearing of the king, and Kaahumanu regarded the moment as auspicious for committing him to some flagrant and public act of hostility to the tabu. Both she and Keopuolani, the queen-mother, had been secretly violating it, since the death of Kamehameha I., by eating of foods interdicted to their sex, and to screen themselves from exposure it was necessary that the religious system should be destroyed of which the tabu was the vital force. This could be accomplished only through the united efforts of the king and high-priest. Hewahewa was prepared to do his part as the religious head of the kingdom, but the young king, notwithstanding the pressure that had been brought to bear upon him by Kaahumanu and a few of the leading chiefs of his court, was still undecided.

A feast was prepared in honor of the king's return to Kailua. In accordance with native custom, separate tables for the sexes were spread, and a number of foreigners were present as the invited guests of Kaahumanu. During the afternoon Liholiho, in response to well-devised banters, had been induced to drink and smoke with the female members of his family. This was a favorable beginning, and, farther emboldened by his mother, who deliberately ate a banana in his presence and drank the milk of a cocoanut, he declared that he would openly set the tabu at defiance during the approaching feast.

It was feared that his courage would fail, and he was not left to himself for a moment until he led the way to the feast. His step was unsteady, and his face wore a troubled expression as he proceeded to the pavilion, accompanied by Kaahumanu, Keopuolani and other members of the royal household. As they separated to take seats at their respective tables, the queen-mother gave Liholiho a look of encouragement, and Kaahumanu said to him in a low tone:

"If you have the courage of your father, this will be a great day for Hawaii."

The king made no reply, for at that moment his eyes fell upon wooden images of Ku and Lono, on opposite sides of the entrance, and he stepped briskly past them and seated himself at the head of one of the tables. The sight of the idols almost unnerved him, and some of the guests observed that his hand trembled as he raised to his lips and drained a vessel of what seemed to be strong liquor.

The guests were all seated. Hewahewa rose, and, glancing at the troubled face of the king, lifted his hands and said with firmness: "One and all, may we eat in peace, and in our hearts give thanks to the one and only god of all."

The words of the high-priest restored the sinking courage of the king. He rose from his seat, deliberately walked to one of the tables reserved for the women, and seated himself beside his mother. During the strange proceeding not a word was spoken, not a morsel touched. Some believed him to be intoxicated; others were sure that he was insane. Since the age of Wakea no one had so defied the gods and lived. Many natives rose from the tables, and horror took the place of astonishment when Liholiho, encouraged by his mother, began to freely partake of the food prepared for the women. Interdicted fish, meats and fruits were then brought to the tables of the women by order of the king, who ate from their plates and drank from their vessels.

Now satisfied that the king was acting deliberately and with the approval of the most influential dignitaries of the kingdom, including the supreme high-priest, a majority of the chiefs present promptly followed the example of their sovereign, and an indescribable scene ensued. "The tabu is broken! the tabu is broken!" passed from lip to lip, swelling louder and louder as it went, until it reached beyond the pavilion. There it was taken up in shouts by the multitude, and was soon wafted on the winds to the remotest corners of Kona. Feasts were at once provided, and men and women ate together indiscriminately. The tabu foods of palace and temple were voraciously eaten by the masses, and thousands of women for the first time learned the taste of flesh and fruits which had tempted their mothers for centuries.

At the conclusion of the royal feast a still greater surprise bewildered the people. "We have made a bold beginning," said Hewahewa to the king, thus adroitly assuming a part of the responsibility; "but the gods and heiaus cannot survive the death of the tabu."

"Then let them perish with it!" exclaimed Liholiho, now nerved to desperation at what he had done. "If the gods can punish, we have done too much already to hope for grace. They can but kill, and we will test their powers by inviting the full measure of their wrath."

To this resolution the high-priest gave his ready assent, and orders were issued at once for the destruction of the gods and temples throughout the kingdom. Resigning his office, Hewahewa was the first to apply the torch, and in the smoke of burning heiaus, images and other sacred property, beginning on Hawaii and ending at Niihau, suddenly passed away a religious system which for fifteen hundred years or more had shaped the faith, commanded the respect and received the profoundest reverence of the Hawaiian people. No creed was offered by the iconoclasts in lieu of the system destroyed by royal edict, and until the arrival of the first Christian missionaries, in March of the year following, the people of the archipelago were left without a shadow of religious restraint or guidance.

II.

While the abolition of the tabu system received the universal approval of the masses, the destruction of the gods and temples met with very considerable remonstrance and opposition. It was believed by many that the priesthood might be preserved without the tabu, and that the king had transcended his sovereign power in striking down both at a single blow. Hence many gods were saved from the burning temples, and thousands refused to relinquish the faith in which they had been reared. Deprived of their occupations, the priests denounced the destruction of the heiaus, and it was not long before a formidable conspiracy against the government was organized on Hawaii, under the leadership of Kekuaokalani, a chief of rare accomplishments and a cousin of the king. Defection appeared at the court, and several chiefs of distinction gave their support to the revolutionary movement.

However it may be regarded in the light of its results, on the part of Kekuaokalani the rebellion was a brave and conscientious defence of the religion of his fathers. He raised the standard of revolt within a day's march of Kailua, and invited to its support all who condemned the action of Liholiho in decreeing the destruction of the national religion. He scorned all compromises and concessions, and but for the firearms of the whites would doubtless have wrested the sceptre from his royal cousin.

It has been asserted that Kekuaokalani was ambitious and availed himself of the discontent created by the antireligious decrees of Liholiho as a possible means of seizing the reins of government. This assumption is not sustained either by the words or acts of the unfortunate chief. The ambassadors sent to him after the first skirmish of the conflict reported that he declined all terms of peaceful settlement. This, however, was not the case. What he demanded was that Liholiho should withdraw his edicts against the priesthood, permit the rebuilding of the temples, and dismiss Kalaimoku as prime minister and Kaahumanu as chief counselor of the government. These conditions were declined, and the ambassadors returned with the story that they had offered to leave the question of religion entirely with the people, but that Kekuaokalani would have nothing but war. A correct statement of what occurred at the interview would doubtless have weakened the royal cause, and was therefore withheld. After the resignation of Hewahewa as high-priest the position devolved upon Kekuaokalani by right of precedence, and, believing in the sanctity of his gods, as a brave man he could not do less than take up arms in their defence.

No characters in Hawaiian history stand forth with a sadder prominence, or add a richer tint to the vanishing chivalry of the race, than Kekuaokalani and his courageous and devoted wife, Manono, the last defenders in arms of the Hawaiian gods. They saw all that the light around them presented, but the only gods known to them were those of their fathers, and they died in a futile effort to protect them. They were brave, noble and conscientious, and the cause in which they perished cannot detract from the grandeur or dim the glory of the sacrifice.

In the veins of Kekuaokalani ran the best blood both of Hawaii and Oahu. He was a nephew of Kamehameha I., and his strain was even superior in rank to that of his distinguished uncle. His great-grandmother was Kamakaimoku, a princess of Oahu, who became the wife of Kalaninuiamamao, one of the sons of Keawe, king of Hawaii, and the mother of Kalaniopuu, grandfather of Keopuolani, mother of Liholiho. One of the full sisters of Kalaniopuu was Manona, the grandmother of Kekuaokalani.

One of the early wives of Kamehameha I. was Kalola, a chiefess of Hawaii. She subsequently became the wife of Kekuamanoha, a younger brother of Kahekili, king of Maui, and the mother of Manono, wife of Kekuaokalani. As the mother of Manono was a daughter of Kumukoa, one of the sons of Keawe, king of Hawaii, and her father was a prince of Maui, she was not only of high rank, but was related in blood both to her husband and the reigning family.

Kekuaokalani is referred to by tradition as one of the most imposing chiefs of his day. He was more than six and a half feet in height, perfect in form, handsome in feature and noble in bearing. Brave, sagacious and magnetic, he possessed the requirements of a successful military leader; but as war had practically ceased with the conquest of the group by Kamehameha I., and he had little taste for the frivolities of the court, where he might have worn out his life in honored idleness, he turned his attention to the priesthood. Beginning at the bottom, with patient application he passed through the intervening degrees until he stood beside the high-priest, fully his equal in learning, and more than his peer in devotion to his calling. He mastered the chronological meles of the higher priesthood and the esoteric lore and secret symbols of the temple, and with the death of Hewahewa it was the universal expectation that the duties of the high-priesthood would devolve upon him. In disposition he was humane, charitable and unselfish, and, appreciating the nobility of his character, his wife worshipped him almost as a god. In return he bestowed upon her the full measure of his affection, and the waters of their lives flowed peacefully on together until the grave engulfed them both.

This was the character of the sturdy chief around whom the friends of the dethroned gods of Hawaii began to rally. He counseled peace and submission so long as he could find listeners among the disaffected, but in the end he was forced into the revolt and became the leader of the movement.

He was present at the royal feast at Kailua when Liholiho publicly violated the tabu and decreed the destruction of the temples. He saw Hewahewa, the venerable high-priest, who had been to an extent his religious guide and instructor, cast the first brand upon the heiau where they had so often worshipped together and sought the counsels of the gods. At first all this seemed to be a horrible dream, but the burning temples and frantic rejoicings of the populace soon convinced him that it was a bewildering reality, and he threw himself to the earth and prayed that his sight might be blasted, that he might witness no farther the sacrilegious acts of the people.

"Liholiho's brain is on fire with strong drink, and he may be urged to do anything," thought Kekuaokalani; "but Hewahewa—it must be that he is insane, and it is my duty to speak with him."

He sought and found the high-priest, and learned to his great grief that Hewahewa was not only sound in mind, but was in thorough accord with the king in his determination to destroy the temples and repudiate the priesthood.

"And you, a high-priest of the blood of Paao, advise this!" said Kekuaokalani, bitterly.

"I advise it," was the calm reply of Hewahewa; "but I am no longer the high-priest of Hawaii; the king has been so notified."

"Then here and now do I assume the vacant place," returned Kekuaokalani, promptly.

"By whose appointment?" inquired Hewahewa.

"By the will of the outraged gods whose temples are turning to ashes around us!" replied Kekuaokalani, with energy. "They will teach me my duty, even should they fail to visit vengeance upon their betrayers!"

With these words Kekuaokalani turned and walked away. His heart was filled with anguish, and the shouts of the people drove him almost to despair. Reaching the pavilion, he lifted and placed upon his shoulder the prostrate and mutilated image of Lono that had stood beside the entrance, and with the precious burden strode gloomily and defiantly past the palace and disappeared.

For a month or more nothing was heard of Kekuaokalani at the court. Meantime, the work of destruction continued, and the smoke of burning temples rose everywhere throughout the group. At length word reached Kailua that some of the priesthood, sustained by a number of influential chiefs, were inciting a revolt in South Kono. Little attention was paid to the report until it was learned that Kekuaokalani had accepted the leadership of the movement. This alarmed the court, and a council of chiefs was called. Discussion developed the prevailing opinion that the threatened uprising was merely a local disturbance that could be quelled without difficulty, and Liholiho's apprehensions were further relieved by the assurance of one of the chiefs that, with the assistance of forty warriors, he would undertake to bring Kekuaokalani a prisoner to Kailua within three days.

"Not with forty times forty!" said Hewahewa, earnestly. Better than any one else he understood and appreciated the lofty courage of Kekuaokalani, and was too generous to listen to its disparagement without protest. "No, not with forty times forty!" he continued. "Without Kekuaokalani the revolt will amount to nothing; with him, it means war."

"Then war let it be, since he invites it!" exclaimed Kalaimoku.

"But may he not be persuaded to peace?" inquired the king, addressing the question, apparently, to Hewahewa.

"Undoubtedly," replied the latter, "if we are prepared to accept his conditions."

"What, think you, would be the conditions?" returned the king.

"The restoration of the tabu and the rebuilding of the temples," was the deliberate answer of Hewahewa.

The king was silent; but before the council dissolved it was understood that a force would be sent against the rebels at once, and for a week or more preparations for the campaign were in progress, under the supervision of Kalaimoku. Everything at length being in readiness, the royal army, numbering, it is presumed, not less than fifteen hundred warriors, some of them bearing firearms, moved southward from Kailua in the direction of Kaawaloa, where had been established the rebel headquarters.

Having accepted the leadership of the rebellion, and regarding himself as a champion selected by the gods for their defence, Kekuaokalani vitalized the movement with an energy and enthusiasm which soon brought the people to its support in large numbers, and the winter solstice found him in command of an army large enough to inspire him with a reasonable hope of success.

The five intercalated days between the winter solstice and the beginning of the new year had from time immemorial been set apart as a season of tabu, dedicated to festivities in honor of Lono, one of the Hawaiian trinity. In the midst of the general religious demoralization Kekuaokalani devoted to the season its customary observances—the last yearly festival ever authoritatively given to Lono in the group.

The movements of the government were regularly and rapidly reported to Kekuaokalani, and when the royal troops left Kailua he was prepared to meet them. Through his efforts a heiau near Kaawaloa had escaped destruction. Thither he repaired, and, offering sacrifices to the gods, prayed that they would manifest their power by giving him victory.

He did not await the assault of the royal forces. Leaving Kaawaloa, he attacked and defeated their advance not far north of that place, throwing the entire army into confusion. Satisfied with the success, he returned to Kaawaloa.

News of the repulse reaching Kailua, a consultation was called by the king, and Kalaimoku urged the prompt advance of reinforcements by land and sea, and an immediate and overwhelming attack upon the rebels at Kaawaloa, rightly claiming that every day would add to the strength of the insurgents under the inspiration of the slight victory they had achieved.

This advice was accepted, and every available force was immediately sent to the front, including a squadron of double canoes under the command of Kaahumanu and Kalakua, one of them carrying a mounted swivel in charge of a foreigner.

Uncertain as to the strength of the rebels, and by no means confident of the results of a struggle which had opened in favor of his enemies, Liholiho advised a resort to peaceful negotiations before staking everything on the chances of battle. Hoapili, who stood in the capacity of husband to the queen-mother, and Naihe, hereditary national counselor and orator, were selected as ambassadors to confer with Kekuaokalani, and Keopuolani volunteered to accompany them.

Reaching the camp of the insurgents, the ambassadors were graciously received by Kekuaokalani, and used every means to effect an amicable settlement of the difficulties that had brought two hostile armies face to face; but nothing satisfactory could be accomplished. They were not authorized to offer such terms as Kekuaokalani felt that he could consistently accept, inasmuch as they failed to embrace either the restoration of the tabu or the rebuilding of the temples. Naihe offered to leave the question of religion optional with the insurgents. To this proposal Kekuaokalani bitterly replied:

"You offer the scales of the fish after you have picked the bones. As they are without temples, where would they worship? As they are without altars, where would they sacrifice? As they are without the tabu, what to them would be sacred and acceptable to the gods?"

"Then must we take back the word that Kekuaokalani will have nothing but war?" said Keopuolani, sadly.

"No, honored mother of princes," replied Kekuaokalani, in a tone so solemn and impressive that his listeners stood awed in his presence. "Say, rather, that Kekuaokalani, the last high-priest, it may be, of Hawaii, is prepared to die in defence of the gods to whose service he has devoted his life. If they are omnipotent, as he believes them to be, their temples will rise again; if not, he is more than willing to hide his disappoint-ment in the grave!"

Naihe was his uncle; Kamakaimoku was the great-grand-mother both of Keopuolani and himself, and the king was his cousin. As a condition of peace he demanded the recall of the edicts against the tabu and the temples. As this could not be conceded, the ambassadors appealed to his relationship with themselves and the royal family; but he could not be moved. "We are proud of our blood," he said to Keopuolani, "but who but the gods made kings of our ancestors?"

Finding that nothing could be effected, the ambassadors withdrew with tokens of mutual regret, and were safely and respectfully escorted beyond the rebel lines. The reports they allowed to be circulated on their return, that Kekuaokalani had refused to consider any terms of peace, and that they had narrowly escaped with their lives, were inventions employed to mislead and exasperate the royal army.

With the departure of the ambassadors Manono sought her husband to learn the results of the conference. The infor-mation that no agreement had been reached did not surprise her. For weeks past all the auguries had indicated blood, and the night before the alae had screamed in the palms behind her hut.

"Thank the gods for the omen!" said Kekuaokalani.

"But the voice of the alae is a presage of evil," suggested Manono.

"Only to those who do evil," replied the chief. "The fate of the gods, whose battles we fight, is shaped by themselves."

"Have you no fear of the result?" inquired Manono.

"I fear nothing," was the reply; "but the thought has

sometimes come to me of late that the gods are reserving for Liholiho and his advisers a punishment greater than I may be able to inflict. Should that be so, I am obstructing with spears the path of their vengeance, and will be sacrificed."

"The will of the gods be done!" said Manono, devoutly. "But, whatever may be the fate of Kekuaokalani, Manono will share it."

"Brave Manono!" exclaimed the husband, with emotion. "If the gods so will it we will die together!"

That night Kekuaokalani took up his line of march for Kailua, determined to give battle to the royal forces wherever he might encounter them. He moved near the coast, and the next morning the hostile armies met at Kuamoo. Arranging his forces in order of battle, Kekuaokalani sent to the front a number of newly-decorated gods in the charge of priests, and, in turn addressing the several divisions, conjured them in impassioned language to defend the gods of their fathers.

Kalaimoku commanded the royal army in person. The battle opened in favor of the rebels, and with them would have been the victory but for the great superiority of the royalists in firearms. At a critical juncture a battalion of musketeers, some of whom were foreigners, charged the rebel centre, when the division gave way in something of a panic, and soon the entire rebel forces were in retreat. Retiring to the adjacent seaside, under cover of a stone wall they made a successful resistance for some time; but the squadron of double canoes already referred to, under the command of Kaahumanu and Kalakua, enfiladed the position with musketry and a mounted swivel, and the insurgents abandoned the unequal struggle, the most of them scattering and seeking shelter in the neighboring hills.

Although wounded early in the action, Kekuaokalani gallantly kept the field. Everywhere was his tall form seen moving throughout the conflict, rallying and cheering his followers, while at his side fought the brave Manono. He finally fell with a musket-ball through his heart. With a wild scream of despair Manono sprang to his assistance, and the next moment a bullet pierced her temple, and she fell dead across the body of her dying husband. Kalaimoku was the first to approach, and gazing long upon the noble features of Kekuaokalani, grand even in death, turned to his followers and said: "Truly, since the days of Keawe a grander Hawaiian has not lived!"

Thus died the last great defenders of the Hawaiian gods. They died as nobly as they had lived, and were buried together where they fell on the field of Kuamoo.

Small bodies of religious malcontents were subdued at Waimea and one or two other points, but the hopes and struggles of the priesthood virtually ended with the death of Kekua-okalani.

THE TOMB OF PUUPEHE

Sailing along the lee-shore or southwest coast of Lanai, a huge block of red lava, sixty feet in diameter and eighty or more feet in height, is discerned standing out in the sea, and detached from the mainland some fifty or sixty fathoms. The sides are precipitous, offering no possible means of ascent, and against it the waves dash in fury, and in the niches of its storm-worn angles the birds of ocean build their nests. Observed from the overhanging bluff of the neighboring shore, on the summit of the lonely column is seen a small enclosure formed by a low but well-defined stone wall. This is known as "The tomb of Puupehe"—the last resting-place of one of the most beautiful of the daughters of Maui, whose body was buried there by her distracted husband and lover, Makakehau, a warrior of Lanai. How the summit was reached by the lover with his precious burden is a mystery, but the wall is still there to show that the ascent was made in some manner, and tradition assumes that it was through the agency of supernatural forces.

Puupehe was the daughter of Uaua, a petty chief of Maui, and Makakehau won her, it is related without detail, as the joint prize of love and war. How this could have occurred it is difficult to imagine, since Lanai was always a dependency of Maui in the past, and no direct wars between the two islands are mentioned by tradition. It may therefore be inferred that she was the spoil of some private predatory expedition, and that the efforts of the young warrior to jealously seclude her from the gaze of men were prompted not more by the infatuations of her beauty than the fear that she might be recaptured.

However this may have been, they are described in the Kanikau, or "Lamentation of Puupehe," as mutually captive to each other in the bonds of love. The maiden was a sweet flower of Hawaiian beauty. Her glossy brown and spotless body "shone like the clear sun rising out of Heleakala." Her flowing hair, bound by wreaths of pikaki blossoms, streamed forth as she ran "like the surf-crests scudding before the wind," and the starry eyes of the daughter of Uaua so dazzled the youthful brave that he was called Makakehau, or "Misty Eyes."

Fearing that the radiant beauty of his captive might cause her to be coveted by some of the chiefs of the land, he said to her: "We love each other well. Let us go to the clear waters of Kalulu. There we will fish together for the kala and bonita, and there will I spear the turtle. I will hide you, O light of my heart! in the cave of Malauea. Or we will dwell together in the great ravine of Palawai, where we will eat the young of the uwau, and bake them in the ti leaf with the sweet pala root. The ohelo berries of the Kuahiwa will refresh us, and we will drink of the cool waters of Maunalei. I will thatch a hut in the thicket of Kaohai, and we will love on till the stars die."

The meles tell of their loves in the Pulou Ravine, where they caught the bright iwi birds and scarlet apapani. How sweet were their joys in the maia groves of Waiakeakua, where the lovers saw naught so beautiful as themselves! But the misty eyes were soon to be made dimmer by weeping, and dimmer till the drowning brine should shut out their light for ever.

Makakehau left his love one day in the cave of Malauea, while he went to the mountain to fill the huawai with sweet water. This cavern yawns at the base of the cliff overlooking the rock of Puupehe. The sea surges far within, but there is an inner space or chamber which the expert swimmer can reach, and where Puupehe had often found seclusion, and baked the honu, or sea-turtle, for her absent lover.

This was the season for the kona, the terrific storm that comes up from the equator, and hurls the billows of ocean with increased violence against the southern shores of the Hawaiian Islands. Makakehau beheld from the rocky springs of Pulou the vanguard of an approaching kona—scuds of rain and thick mist rushing with a howling wind across the round valley of Palawai. He knew the storm would fill the cave with a wild and sudden rush of waters, and destroy the life of his beautiful Puupehe.

Every moment was precious. He flung aside his cala-bashes of water, and at the top of his speed started down the mountain. With mighty and rapid strides he crossed the great valley, where he met the coming storm in its fury. Over the rim he dashed with an agonized heart, and down the ragged slope of the kula to the shore, which the waves were already lashing in a voice of thunder.

The sea was up, indeed! The yeasty foam of surging, wind-rent billows whitened the cliffs, and the tempest cho-russed the mad anthem of the battling waves. Oh! where should Misty Eyes seek for his love in the blinding storm?

A rushing mountain of sea fills the mouth of the cave of Malauea, and the pent air within hurls back the invading tor-rent with a stubborn roar, blowing outward great streams of spray. It is a savage war of the elements—a battle of the forces of nature well calculated to thrill with pleasure the hearts of strong men. But a lover looking into the seething gulf of the whirlpool—what would be to him the sublime conflict? what to see amid the boiling brine the upturned face and tender body of the idol of his heart?

Others might agonize on the brink, but Misty Eyes

sprang into the dreadful caldron and snatched his lifeless love from the jaws of an ocean grave.

The next day fishermen heard the lamentation of Makakehau, and the women of the valley came down and wailed over Puupehe. They wrapped her body in bright, new kapa, and covered it with garlands of fragrant nauu. They prepared it for interment, and were about to place it in the burial ground of Manele; but Makakehau prayed that he might be left alone one night more with his lost love, and the request was not refused.

When the women returned the morning following they found neither corpse nor wailing lover. At length, looking toward the rock of Puupehe, they discovered Makakehau at work on the lofty apex of the lone sea-tower. The wondering people of the island watched him with amazement from the neighboring cliffs, but, heedless of their observation, he continued his labors. Some sailed around the base of the column in their canoes, but could discover no means of ascent. Every face of the rock was either perpendicular or overhanging.

The conviction then became general—since there seemed to be no other possible explanation—that some sympathizing akua, or spirit, had responded to the prayer of Makakehau, and assisted him in reaching the summit of the tower with the body of his dead bride; and in this form has tradition brought down the touching story.

Makakehau finished his labors. He laid his love in a grave prepared by his own hands, placed the last stone upon it, and then stretched out his arms and thus wailed for Puupehe:

"Where are you, O Puupehe?
Are you in the cave of Malauea?

Shall I bring you sweet water,
The water of the fountain?
Shall I bring the uwau,
The pala and ohelo?
Are you baking the honu?
And the red, sweet hala?
Shall I pound the kalo of Maui?
Shall we dip in the gourd together?
The bird and the fish are bitter,
And the mountain water is sour.
I shall drink it no more;
I shall drink with Aipuhi,
The great shark of Manele."

Ceasing his sad wail, Makakehau gazed for a moment upon the grave where were buried the light and hope of his life, and then leaped from the rock into the boiling surge at its base. His body was crushed in the breakers. The witnesses of the sacrifice secured the mangled remains of the dead lover, and interred them with respect in the kupapau of Manele.

This is the story told by the old bards of Lanai of the lonely rock of Puupehe, and the still inaccessible summit, with the marks of a grave upon it, attests with reasonable certainty that: the mele has something of a foundation in fact.

KAHAVARI, CHIEF OF PUNA

A STORY OF THE VENGEANCE OF THE GODDESS PELE

Between Cape Kumakahi, the extreme eastern point of the island of Hawaii, and the great lava flow of 1840, which burst forth apparently from a long subterranean channel connecting with the crater of Kilauea, and went down to the sea at Nanawale over villages and groves of palms, is a small historic district which, notwithstanding the repeated volcanic disturbances with which it has been convulsed in the past, the chasms with which it has been rent, and the smoke and ashes that have shut out the light of the sun and driven its people to the protection of their temples, still possesses many fertile nooks and natural attractions. Within a few miles of each other, not far inland, are a number of extinct craters; but the rains are abundant in Puna, and spring is eternal, and the vegetation grows rank above hidden patches of lava, and is constantly stretching and deepening its mantle of green over the vitreous rivers of Kilauea and the lower and lesser volcanic vents clinging to its base like so many cauterized ulcers.

The valleys are green in that part of Puna now, and there the banana and the bread-fruit grow, and the ohia and pineapple scent the air. But so has it not always been, for the mango ripens over fields of buried lava, and the palms grow tall from the refilled chasms of dead streams of fire. The depression of Kapoho, now sweet with tropical odors, marks the site of a sunken mountain, and where to-day sleep the quiet waters of a lake once boiled a sea of liquid lava, in a basin broader, perhaps, than the mighty caldron of Kilauea.

We are now about to speak of one of the many irruptions which at intervals in the past poured their desolating torrents of fire through the district, alternately loved and hated by Pele, the dreadful goddess of the volcanoes. In connection with it tradition has brought down a tale combining elements of simplicity and grandeur strikingly characteristic of the mythological legends of Polynesia—legends equaling the Norse in audacity, but lacking the motive and connecting causes of the Greek. They are simply legendary epics, beginning in caprice and abruptly ending, in many instances, in grandest tumult. They are like chapters torn from a lost volume—patches of disturbed elements and gigantic forms and energies clandestinely cut from a passing panorama and placed in the foreground of strange and inharmonious conditions. They embrace gods reminding us of Thor, monsters more hideous than Polyphemus, demi-gods mighty as the son of Thetis, and kings with strains reaching back to the loins of gods; but in motive and action they were independent of, and not unfrequently hostile to, each other. No celestial synod shaped their course or moved them to effort, and to no authority higher than their individual wills were they usually responsible. Many of them were created with no reference to the necessity of their being or the maintenance of divine respect or authority, and not a few seem to have been the creations of accident.

As an example the demi-god Maui may be mentioned. As told by tradition, his principal abode was Hawaii, although his facilities for visiting the other islands of the group will be considered ample when it is stated that he could step from one to another, even from Oahu to Kauai, a distance of seventy miles. When he bathed—and bathing was one of his greatest delights—his feet trod the deepest basins of the ocean and his hair was moistened with the vapor of the clouds. Neither his creator nor the purpose of his creation is mentioned; but he was blest with a wife with proportions, it is presumed, somewhat in keeping with his own, and as an evidence of their attachment it is related that at one time he reached up and seized the sun, and held it for some hours motionless in the heavens, to enable his industrious spouse to complete the manufacture of a piece of kapa upon which she was engaged.

And Kana was another gigantic being of similar proportions. He, too, was partial to Hawaii, and could step from island to island, and frequently stood for his amusement with one foot on Oahu and the other either on Maui or Kauai. Tradition may have confounded these two monsters; but, as Kana was wifeless, we are constrained to regard them as distinct; and, being without the care of a wife, he was enabled to devote his entire attention to himself and the inhabitants of the islands crawling at his feet. Hence, when the king of Kahiki, who was the keeper of the sun, shut its light from the Hawaiians for some trivial offence, Kana waded the ocean to the home of the vindictive monarch, and by threats compelled him to restore the light to the Hawaiian group. This done, he waded back and hung his mantle to dry on Mauna Kea, which was then an active volcano. Another demi-god of the same name is also referred to in some of the early meles of Hawaii. He was the son of Hina, who went with his brother to the rescue of their mother, who had been during their infancy abducted by the son of the king of Molokai. He was endowed by his grandmother, a sorceress from one of the southern islands, with the faculty of so elongating and contracting his person as to be able to pass through the deepest waters with his head at all times above the surface.

The shadows of these and other monsters are seen far back in the past; but human beings of gigantic proportions, of natural birth and claiming no connection with the gods, are mentioned in Hawaiian folk-lore as having lived as late as the beginning of the sixteenth century. Thus, during the reign of Umi, king of Hawaii, whose romantic ascent to the throne is the theme of chant and song, and to whom the past and present dynasties of united Hawaii trace their descent, lived the giant Maukaleoleo. He was one of Umi's warriors, and must have been a mighty host in himself. His measure in feet is not recorded, but he stood upon the ground and plucked cocoanuts from the tallest trees, and once, without wetting his loins, strode out into six fathoms of water and saved the life of his chief. As the traditions relating to Umi are quite elaborate and circumstantial, the existence of Maukaleoleo cannot well be doubted, however greatly we may feel disposed to curtail his proportions.

But, in groping among these monsters of the Hawaiian past, we have been led somewhat from the story of the irruption in Puna, to which reference has been made. However, as pertinent to it, and to the goddess whose wrath invoked it, it may be mentioned that many centuries ago a family of gods and goddesses came to Hawaii from Tahiti and took possession of the volcanic mountains of that island. The family consisted of five brothers and nine sisters, of which Pele was the principal deity. The others possessed specific powers and functions, such as controlling the fires, smoke, steam, explosions, etc., of the volcanoes under their supervision. Although they frequently dwelt in other volcanoes, their principal and favorite abode was the crater of Kilauea. Almost without exception they were destructive and merciless. Temples were

erected to Pele in every district menaced by volcanic disturbance, and offerings of fruits, animals, and sometimes of human beings were laid upon her altars and thrown into the crater to secure her favor or placate her wrath. In the legend of
"The Apotheosis of Pele" a more extended reference is made
to the goddess and her family.

With this knowledge of the power and disposition of
Pele, the reader will be prepared for the story of the exhibition of her wrath in Puna, which will now be related nearly
in the language of tradition. The event occurred during the
reign of Kahoukapu, who from about 1340 to 1380 was the
alii-nui, or governing chief, of Hawaii. The chief of the district
of Puna was Kahavari, a young noble distinguished for his
strength, courage and manly accomplishments. How he came
to be chief or governor of Puna is not stated. As his father and
sister lived on Oahu, he was probably a native of that island,
and may have been advanced to his position through military
service rendered the Hawaiian king, since it was customary in
those days, as it was at later periods, for young men of martial tastes to seek adventure and employment at arms with the
kings and chiefs of neighboring islands.

The grass-thatched mansion of the young chief was near
Kapoho, where his wife lived with their two children, Paup-
oulu and Kaohe; and at Kukii, no great distance away, dwelt
his old mother, then on a visit to her distinguished son. As his
taro lands were large and fertile, and he had fish-ponds on the
sea-shore, he entertained with prodigality, and the people of
Puna thought there was no chief like him in all Hawaii.

It was at the time of the monthly festival of Lono. The
day was beautiful. The trade-winds were bending the leaves of
the palms and scattering the spray from the breakers chasing

each other over the reef. A holua contest had been announced between the stalwart young chief and his favorite friend and companion, Ahua, and a large concourse of men, women and children had assembled at the foot of the hill to witness the exciting pastime. They brought with them drums, ohes, uli-lis, rattling gourds and other musical instruments, and while they awaited the coming of the contestants all frolicked as if they were children—frolicked as was their way before the white man came to tell them they were nearly naked, and that life was too serious a thing to be frittered away in enjoyment. They ate ohias, cocoanuts and bananas under the palms, and chewed the pith of sugar-cane. They danced, sang and laughed at the hula and other sports of the children, and grew nervous with enthusiasm when their bards chanted the meles of by-gone years.

The game of holua consists in sliding down a sometimes long but always steep hill on a narrow sledge from six to twelve feet in length, called a papa. The light and polished runners, bent upward at the front, are bound quite closely together, with cross-bars for the hands and feet. With a run at the top of the sliding track, slightly smoothed and sometimes strewn with rushes, the rider throws himself face downward on the narrow papa and dashes headlong down the hill. As the sledge is not more than six or eight inches in width, with more than as many feet in length, one of the principal difficulties of the descent is in keeping it under the rider; the other, of course, is in guiding it; but long practice is required to master the sub-tleties of either. Kahavari was an adept with the papa, and so was Ahua. Rare sport was therefore expected, and the people of the neighborhood assembled almost in a body to witness it.

Finally appearing at the foot of the hill, Kahavari and his

companion were heartily cheered by their good-natured audi-
tors. Their papas were carried by attendants. The chief smiled
upon the assemblage, and as he struck his tall spear into the
ground and divested his broad shoulders of the kihei covering
them, the wagers of fruit and pigs were three to one that he
would reach the bottom first, although Ahua was expert with
the papa, and but a month before had beaten the champion of
Kau on his own ground.

Taking their sledges under their arms, the contestants
laughingly mounted the hill with firm, strong strides, neither
thinking of resting until the top was gained. Stopping for a
moment preparatory to the descent, a comely-looking woman
stepped out from behind a clump of undergrowth and bowed
before them. Little attention was paid to her until she approached still nearer and boldly challenged Kahavari to contest the holua with her instead of Ahua. Exchanging a smile of
amusement with his companion, the chief scanned the lithe
and shapely figure of the woman for a moment, and then exclaimed, more in astonishment than in anger: "What! with a
woman?"

"And why not with a woman, if she is your superior and
you lack not the courage?" was the calm rejoinder.

"You are bold, woman," returned the chief, with something of a frown. "What know you of the papa?"

"Enough to reach the bottom of the hill in front of the
chief of Puna," was the prompt and defiant answer.

"Is it so, indeed? Then take the papa and we will see!"
said Kahavari, with an angry look which did not seem to dis-
turb the woman in the least.

At a motion from the chief, Ahua handed his papa to
the woman, and the next moment Kahavari, with the strange

contestant closely behind him, was dashing down the hill. On, on they went, around and over rocks, at break-neck speed; but for a moment the woman lost her balance, and Kahavari reached the end of the course a dozen paces in advance.

Music and shouting followed the victory of the chief, and, scowling upon the exultant multitude, the woman pointed to the hill, silently challenging the victor to another trial. They mounted the hill without a word, and turned for another start.

"Stop!" said the woman, while a strange light flashed in her eyes. "Your papa is better than mine. If you would act fairly, let us now exchange!"

"Why should I exchange?" replied the chief, hastily. "You are neither my wife nor my sister, and I know you not. Come!" And, presuming the woman was following him, Kahavari made a spring and dashed down the hill on his papa.

With this the woman stamped her foot, and a river of burning lava burst from the hill and began to pour down into the valley beneath. Reaching the bottom, Kahavari rose and looked behind him, and to his horror saw a wide and wild torrent of lava rushing down the hillside toward the spot where he was standing; and riding on the crest of the foremost wave was the woman—now no longer disguised, but Pele, the dreadful goddess of Kilauea—with thunder at her feet and lightning playing with her flaming tresses.

Seizing his spear, Kahavari, accompanied by Ahua, fled for his life to the small eminence of Puukea. He looked behind, and saw the entire assemblage of spectators engulfed in a sea of fire. With terrible rapidity the valleys began to fill, and he knew that his only hope of escape was in reaching the ocean, for it was manifest that Pele was intent upon his destruction. He fled to his house, and, passing it without stopping, said farewell to his mother, wife and children, and to his favorite hog Aloipuaa. Telling them that Pele was in pursuit of him with a river of fire, and to save themselves, if possible, by escaping to the hills, he left them to their fate.

Coming to a chasm, he saw Pele pouring down it to cut off his retreat. He crossed on his spear, pulling his friend over after him. At length, closely pursued, he reached the ocean. His brother, discovering the danger, had just landed from his fishing canoe and gone to look after the safety of his family. Kahavari leaped into the canoe with his companion, and, using his spear for a paddle, was soon beyond the reach of the pursuing lava. Enraged at his escape, Pele ran some distance into the water and hurled after him huge stones, that hissed as they struck the waves, until an east wind sprang up and carried him far out to sea.

He first reached the island of Maui, and thence by the way of Lanai found his way to Oahu, where he remained to the end of his days. All of his relatives in Puna perished, with hundreds of others in the neighborhood of Kapoho. But he never ventured back to Puna, the grave of his hopes and his people, for he believed Pele, the unforgiving, would visit the place with another horror if he did.

Pele had come down from Kilauea in a pleasant mood to witness the holua contest; but Kahavari angered her unwittingly, and what followed has just been described.

www.sophenebooks.com

SOPHENE

www.ingramcontent.com/pod-product-compliance
Lightning Source LLC
Chambersburg PA
CBHW020659260626

47157CB00008B/3098